Copyright 2019 Mary Angland

All rights reserved

Mary Angland asserts her moral right

to be identified as the author of this work.

No part of this publication may be reproduced, stored in a

Retrieval system, or transmitted, in any form or in any other means-

by electronic, mechanical, photocopying, recording or otherwise

-without prior written permission.

This book is a work of fiction. Names, characters, places and

incidents either are products of the author's imagination or are

used fictitiously. Any resemblance to actual persons, living or

dead, events or locales is entirely coincidental.

Published by Grey Heron Press

**Dedication.**

*To the indomitable women who instilled in me a love of story- telling and so much more, my mother, Josie and her sister, Maggie, with much love.*

## Acknowledgements:

*To my writing partners and friends, Mary Bradford, Marie O'Halloran and Mary-Anne Bartlett for suggestions, encouragement and keeping me motivated. To Viv Buckley for her wonderful cover design and photograph. To the sounding boards, Sheila O'Connor, Lisa Egan, Marguerite O'Connor.*

*To all, mile buíochas*

# Table of Contents

Acknowledgements: 2

Maggie May 4

The Laughing Boy 10

Dreaming Dreams 17

Isaac's Farmhouse 20

The Cry of the Curlew 25

Sonny 33

Sanctuary 37

Waiting 42

Miners' Alley 45

The Witching Hour 50

Epiphany 57

Rubber Man 60

Chrissie 66

Nothing is, But What is Not 68

The Country Boy 79

Jimmy's Cross 83

A Night in September 90

The Doormat 96

Turn the Ship and Away We Go 98

The Homecoming 104

The Grafter 110

Voices from Afar 112

Wedding preparations 116

# Maggie May

It is summer. I am nine years old. I run out the gate of the village school and swerve to avoid a cow-pat in the middle of the street. I pass *Bunty Archibold*'s dark little shop before turning down *Cobblers' Lane* and taking the short cut home through the quarry. Here, the sun plays hide and seek as the line of old trees open and close around me. I hear the padding of my bare feet on the dusty path. My chest feels too small for the giant thump, thump of my heart, see -sawing up and down in my throat.

I stumble around the creamery bend, breath and heart jostling in my chest. In front of me, our narrow little road spreads away in a jumble of jumping shadows and dancing light. I see the road outside my gate and my breath strangles in my throat. I stumble on again.

I came into the world just before midnight in the tiny, back bedroom of the family cottage on February 9th 1930. At almost that exact moment in the creamery, a few hundred yards away, Thade Bob Carroll from the village was torn out of it. No one ever knew what exactly happened but around the time Mamma was holding me in her arms for the first time, Thade Bob lost his footing and fell, entangling himself on one of the creamery's permanently, revolving wheels and there, with nobody to hear, he screamed himself into silence. In the dark winter nights, the great shadow of the creamery loomed out of the blackness at the end of our road. Going to sleep sometimes, even though I'd never known him, I would see behind my tightly clenched eyelids, the bloody image of Thade Bob, mangled on the mighty wheel and I'd imagine his cries, tumbling uselessly behind him, in the great empty creamery.

I was christened Margaret Mary but no one ever called me that, except Auntie Bridie, Mamma' stuck-up older sister. I was always Maggie and sometimes when Mamma rocked me on her lap, she called me Maggie May. Until I was nine years old my childhood was carefree, the days turning over one on the other in a blaze of light and colour.

I ran barefoot through the fields with my sister Hannah, two years older than me, eating berries and catching minnows in jam jars in the river straggling lazily by the end of the village. We built cabby houses under the shade of the horse-chestnut in the haggart and fought furiously over treasure troves of old tins and jam- jars. In the spring and summer, we rode imaginary horses up-river to catch the murderous baddies holed up in the dark sprawl of tangled woods that surrounded the village.

Our little village had a comforting sameness. In the summer, the farmers came in from the countryside, bringing their churns of milk to the creamery on ponies and carts. Wandering beggars like old Mrs Hourigan and Paddy One Paw slipped into our lives in the autumn, disappearing when the spring sunshine shyly peeped over Daly's Hill and smiled down over the village. Paddy One Paw camped beside the hedgerows in the Old Road just off the village. He had a little black and white terrier called Patch and when Paddy clicked the fingers on his one hand, Patch shot up on his little hind legs and lurched along the road for a few seconds - looking remarkably like Miss Deakin, who had retired back to the village from America. Every Sunday, she tottered, lollipop stick legs on pink sandals, up the aisle for communion. Every week, from the front seat of the gallery, Hannah and I held our breaths as we watched her and were always disappointed when she and her pink sandals returned in one piece to the safety of her pew. A little tumble would have created a bit of excitement to help us through *Canon Browne*'s long mumbled Mass.

The languid wave of village life was ruffled now and again when older boys and girls left to go to England or America. Sometimes their mothers called in for a cup of tea and sat on the stool by the old bellows and cried, while Mamma's gentle voice soothed and her soft hands patted bent backs. I hovered around Mamma then, clutching her skirts tightly in small sweaty hands, maddened with a terror I couldn't understand. I was always glad when these sad mothers left and Mamma shushed me and put me on her lap.

"Why did Patie go away, Mamma, when it makes his mammy cry?"

"To get work, a stór, and then he can send a bit of money back to his mammy so she won't have to work so hard anymore."

"I don't want to go away, Mamma, when I'm big. I want to stay here with you. I'm never going to leave you, Mamma, never, ever."

I was never very close to Dadda, a thin man, who spoke little and who wore his cloth cap pulled down over his eyes like he wanted to hide from people. For as long as I remember, my world danced around the sun that was Mamma. Tiny and slim, she had black curly hair and loved to sing. I loved when she whirled Hannah and me round and round the small kitchen, while we screamed with delight. Her favourite song was very sad though. It was all about saying goodnight to a girl called *Irene* but she could only be seen in dreams because she wasn't really there. I didn't really understand what it meant at all.

In winter nights around the kitchen fire, Mamma told us marvellous spell- weaving tales of flying shawls and crafty goblins and magic beds that came alive at night and travelled through the sky. The only light we had was from the open fire and Hannah and I shivered with delicious terror when Mamma whispered tales of the Hairy Boy O, a giant, who lived in nearby Gleann na gCapall. We'd never seen him but we knew that he hid behind ditches, waiting to pounce on travellers out alone at night. He'd take all their belongings, Mamma said and then put a spell on them so that they'd remember nothing at all of what had happened and spend the rest of their lives going around the countryside, gibbering like idiots. When the story ended, her voice died away, first into a whisper and then a silence and when I chanced to peep out from half closed eyes, I saw winking, melting stripples of light leaping and dancing around the walls of our little kitchen.

"The fire is going out," Mamma would say slyly with a sideways look at us. "Will ye go out for a gabháil of cipíns to keep it going till Dadda comes home from work?"

Then the delicious waves of shivery terror spread up from my toes and with a shriek, I'd fling myself onto her lap. Grasping the black curls at the back of her neck, I'd hide my face in the comforting blackness of the old shawl she always wore around the house.

It was summer when Mamma changed. She didn't play with us much anymore or tell us her wonderful stories and she was tired all the time. She stopped singing and there was no more twirling and dancing around the kitchen. Instead, sitting by the bellows, Mamma would put her hands to her head and rock gently back and forth. Sometimes, she didn't seem to realise that Hannah and I were even there.

"You never tell us stories anymore, Mamma. Why don't you tell us stories anymore?"

"Come here so, a stór, and I'll tell you a story now."

Then she rubs my face and I snuggle into her lap and soon we're on a flying bed high over the village. Looking down, I can see all these little moving dots. But I know they're really people and above Mamma and me, high in the sky, are all sorts of animals. There are elephants and monkeys and even lions and tigers and they're all racing and tumbling across the sky. They aren't really animals though, they're fluffy, roundy clouds but Mamma and me pretend they are animals and that they are chasing us on our flying bed.

And all the time Mamma is talking, I'm softly rubbing the big lump on her forehead under her black curls. It's soft and roundy and big like the clouds above our flying bed. It's like the lump I got when I fell from the big tree in the haggart but Mamma didn't fall from the tree. She says the lump just grew all by itself and then she says we won't talk about the old lump anymore because we're just above the coast of England now and we must watch out for the king in case we miss him. She said millions and millions of people live in England and if we don't watch very carefully, we might miss him in the big crowd.

Just after Christmas, sour-faced Auntie Bridie, Mamma's sister and her husband Jack came down from their tin- roofed house on the hill. Once, we were frightened when we overheard Aunt Bridie shouting at Dadda in the kitchen, and later when Hannah asked her what TB was, she gave her a crack across the face and made her nose bleed. Hannah had a big red streak down one side of her face for ages but she never cried. She wouldn't give Auntie Bridie the soot of it, she said. We were fond of Uncle Jack though, who had a short leg and who gave us boiled sweets sometimes, when Auntie Bridie wasn't looking.

Every day Hannah and I raced home from school taking the short cut down by Bunty's shop and through the quarry. I'd be praying silently to all the saints and my guardian angel that Mamma would be up and sitting by the fire when we got home. And when I ran through the front door into the shadows of the kitchen, and saw her sitting by the bellows, my heart leapt and the sun lit up the small room like a flickering candle.

"I'll be grand as soon as the summer comes," Mamma promised us, 'shure, I'm getting a bit stronger already."

But she wasn't.

In bed at night, Hannah and I cuddled up to each other and stared into the darkness, hearts pounding with terror. We clutched hands tightly as we listened to the thin voice that had once soared and tumbled with us in the magic bed.

I stumble around the creamery bend, breath and heart jostling in my chest. In front of me, our narrow little road spreads away in a jumble of jumping shadows and dancing light. I see the road outside our cottage and my breath strangles in my throat. I reach the gate just as Dadda brings Mamma out from the back bedroom. A stick in a faded blue nightdress and the holey cardigan she always wears in bed. And when Mamma sees me, she stops and leans against Dadda and holds out her arms. Her hands touching my face are gentle. They tremble on my skin like butterfly wings. But then Mamma starts to cry. And Dadda puts his arm around her and slowly carries her away from me and out through the small wooden gate. And Mamma half turns her head to look at me. I try to run to her but my feet won't move. Then, then, I can't see Mamma anymore and Dadda stands beside the gate as the big van carries Mamma slowly away down towards the creamery and disappears around the bend in the road.

Mamma, Mamma!

I run to Dadda and hold on to his coat, but he just stands and looks down the long empty road. And when I look at his face, I have to bend over and a spray of grey water and soft pellets like sour milk spurt from my mouth. I look at the pellets lying there on the road. And I feel myself getting smaller and smaller. And inside me, Mamma is a long silent scream, forever lost in the criss-crossed pattern of ambulance tyres in the flaky dust beneath my feet.

## The Laughing Boy

At 8am precisely, the Crossley Tender, drove out through the main gates of the barracks in the small garrison town of Tullybawn, and immediately turned left in the direction of Curramore village, just under three miles away to the west. As it belched its way in a cloud of blue smoke along the small country road, the Black and Tans sitting at the back of the lorry were tense and silent. The journey from Tullybawn to Glenlara Barracks was barely twenty miles but the route was a soldier's nightmare, taking in, not only the village of Curramore, but the deep winding glen of Gleann na gCapall or Glen of the Horses, as the Tans knew it. From the minute the lorry entered the glen from the Curramore direction until it emerged onto the Glenlara side, it would travel through almost three miles of narrow winding road, bordered on one side by high wooded slopes and on the other by a deep ravine with a small fast flowing river. Sporadic rebel activity had been reported in the Curramore area over the last few weeks and HQ were determined to stamp out any potential trouble by sending frequent high visibility patrols out around the countryside

The small village of Curramore slumbered in the warm glow of the June sunshine. It was still too early for many to be about. Old Patsy Connors, always first to appear in the street, drew down a bucket of water from the village pump, just a stone's throw from the forge. As early as it was, wisps of smoke climbed leisurely from the chimney. Inside, the forge was full of dancing shadows though it would be a while yet before the sun swept into all the dusty corners. Christy O'Connell, bathed in a halo of sparks, hammered at the red hot piece of steel on the anvil. Drops of sweat glistened like marbles on his forehead, even though he wore nothing but a pair of old woollen trousers and a blackened apron pulled over his bare chest. Outside in the sunlight, a couple of Rhode Island hens pecked half- heartedly along the dusty street and Noonan's old black and white sheep dog sprawled in front of the shop, head buried deep between his front paws.

Private Albert Hawkins, hunched nearest the tailboard of the lorry, rifle in between his knees, felt his bowels move and hoped desperately he wouldn't make a show of himself in front of the others. Already, he could feel the prickling of sweat under his armpits and his skin itched from the cheap khaki cloth. He knew, same as the others, that the patrol could have gone by the high road, around by Daly's Hill and avoided the glen altogether. But Captain Hastings wouldn't hear of it.

'Skulking round the long road, loike we're scared! Scared of these murdering Oirish bastards. No bleeding way!'

His pencil moustache moved up and down as he spoke and little spots of spittle formed like sea spray on his lower lip.

So 'ere we are then, sitting ducks for any Shinner who wants to take a pot shot at us, all because Captain bloody 'astings 'aint got the bloody brains 'e was born with, Albert thought sarcastically.

Old Patsy raised his head. He felt the sweat break out on his body. By the time his shaking hands had closed his cottage door behind him, the Crossley Tender was entering the village. Without reducing speed, it roared like a wounded elephant along the long street, throwing up swirling sprays of dust and scattering the squawking hens in a flurry of indignation and feathers. A small pool of water darkened a patch of ground outside Old Patsy's cottage and inside the old man crossed himself, while Christy in the forge stopped his hammering and listened intently.

'Bastards' he muttered and his hands tightened unconsciously on the hammer. Shifting his head slightly, he spat on the dusty floor and without noticing, let out a long shuddering sigh as he heard the lorry, without once slackening speed, trundle through the village and head in the direction of Gleann na gCapall.

Gradually, the peace of the morning was restored as the engine of the Crossley faded away in the distance and the early morning silence settled like an embrace around the village again.

'Bleeding bastards, all of 'em,' Corporal Whyte said savagely to Albert 'watching from behoind their little windows, 'oping we'll be plugged by their murdering sons and 'usbands. And their wives and bleeding daughters too,' he added 'fer all Oi know.'

Albert said nothing. The lorry entered the glen and he saw the high slopes on his left and the slow snake of water some twenty-five feet below on his right. He clutched his rifle tighter, hands sweaty. He looked around at the men, smelling the fear, saw the darting eyes and jumping Adams' apples.

'Perfect for an ambush, eh.' Whyte gave a nervous giggle.

'Shut th' fuck up', snarled the stocky Tan opposite.

Despite himself, Albert found his mind wandering back to last week's dawn patrol. He remembered Corporal Whyte and some of the others, red faced and sweating, standing up in the lorry as they passed through the countryside, shooting at everything, cows, donkeys and crows, whooping and screaming like madmen and Captain Hastings smiling at their antics, yeah, even encouraging them. Bile rose in his throat as he remembered the slow fall of the old woman, crumpling without a sound on the ground, thin legs sprawled obscenely as the yellow yolk of the broken eggs dribbled away slowly onto the dust.

No wonder they bloody well 'ate us, Albert thought, wot we doing 'ere anyway? We got no roight to be 'ere, no roight at all.

There wasn't a minute of the day when he didn't regret joining up, that he wished he'd never volunteered, never seen that bleeding notice recruiting a new force for Ireland. He'd returned from the Great War a hero but found things in England had changed very quickly. Molly had married. Funny that, he never thought she wouldn't be there for him. Married to Pearson, of all people, with his little shifty eyes, Pearson, who couldn't go to save little Belgium because of his stammer and short leg.

'You wasn't there, Bert,' she'd mumbled tearfully 'I was lonely.'

Suddenly, the heroes of the Great War were yesterday's men, an embarrassment. People's eyes slid away when they saw the broken faces and parents turned their little kids from the sight of empty sleeves and empty trouser legs.

The flu his father had caught in the summer of 1918 had destroyed his lungs. Poor sod, 'e was bleeding lucky to be alive at all.

'I'll be back at work soon as good weather comes round, lad.' Coughing into the ashes, shrunken and beaten, they both knew he would never work again. His mother's silent despairing eyes were almost worse to bear, so when he saw the poster on the tavern wall, looking for men to sign up and keep the peace in Ireland, he thought it an answer to a prayer. Bloody 'ell, he'd signed up like a shot. Ten shillings a day would look after the old people, 'e'd 'ave free board and lodgings and 'e'd be working, could 'old his 'ead up again. Best of all, maybe, he wouldn't have to see Molly every day and …

'Stupid sod,' he mocked himself, looking at the tense faces of the swaying bodies beside him in the lorry, eyes resting on Whyte, stomach straining against the fabric of his tunic. His tongue, a pink slip of raw meat, popped out every few seconds like a snake, and licked his lips before disappearing back into the pink hole again. Albert felt sick. He took his cap off. Christ, it was 'ot. Running his fingers around the rim, he heard Whyte say something to him and turned.

The column had been in the ditch almost three hours now. Thomas groaned and shifted slightly. His feet were cramped and he could feel the vicious stabbing of the pins and needles in his left foot. He glanced at his companion. Young Jamsie looked bad – uneven lines of sweat on his face and his burning eyes sunk back in his head. He hadn't been the same since the column had been forced to spend almost a week sleeping in the open air in mid -April. For almost a week, the Tans had crawled all over the countryside, raiding houses known to be sympathetic to the cause, beating up innocent people, shooting livestock and terrifying everyone.

The lads hadn't dared sleep in any of the safe houses and to make it worse, the nights had been bitterly cold with icy torrential showers. They'd been almost continuously wet and Jamsie picked up a chill, which he'd never managed to shake off. During the last few days, he'd got worse, shivering and feverish but he'd insisted on coming with them. Thomas had reluctantly agreed but looking now at his perspiring face and bloodshot eyes, he bitterly regretted that decision. He swore under his breath and squinted down the valley, sleeping like a twisted, serpent beneath him. Three fields away, a thin wisp of smoke curled lazily from Timmy Ben's cottage. Another hour and then they'd go.

He settled down again. His eyes drifted over the fields below him and when he turned back, the fox was there – standing not ten feet away from them. Christ, she was beautiful. Her russet coat gleamed dully in the sunlight and she held her tail like she was royalty. She raised her head and sniffed and then padded daintily across the grass and with a quick effortless bound, she was over the hedge at the corner of the field and away. He stood up carefully and watched her, mouth slightly open as she glided purposefully through the scrub grass before disappearing over the brow of the hill. Smiling slightly, he hoped Timmy Ben had his hens locked up. He shifted again and squinting upwards, noted the sun was climbing higher. Jaysus it was going to be another scorcher.

He looked down the ditch but could see no one, except Jamsie. He knew they were there though, John and Petie and Mick and Joey waiting his signal. Christ, so many ditches, so many signals, so many killings. He looked back at Jamsie. God, the lad was so bloody young. He'd been like that once, a lifetime ago, in another world. He remembered the laughing lad whirling Katie Barry like a mad spinning top at Hannigans' barn dance and the sweat streaming down Dinny Moloney's broad face as his fingers raced and leapt over the keyboard of his aul squeeze box. For a moment, his face softened but then he tightened his lips. Enough! Thoughts like that made you soft and when you were soft, you made mistakes. Suddenly, his hand clenched as he heard his father's bitter laugh.

'Listen boyo, it matters not one whit whether we're ruled by the English or the Irish. We'll still be struggling to survive and you're a bigger bollox than I took you for, if you believe being ruled by Irishmen is going to make any fecking difference to the likes of us.'

Well, that laughing boy was dead, wandering forever in a grey world of bodies and bullets, a world where you trusted no one except those whose loyalty was proven, like the lads in the ditch beside him. For them, there was no yesterday and no tomorrow. There was only the ditch they were lying in, the next ambush and the winding glen below.

Abruptly, he stopped. Eyes narrowed, body rigid, hands clenched on metal, he scanned the glen spread out underneath him. The hum of an engine, faint at first but getting louder and rougher as he listened. Like a shutter, his eyes narrowed in a straight line from the ditch.

He turned urgently to Jamsie, flapping his hand and pointing. Jamsie nodded quickly and began to crawl rapidly to his right.

By the time, the Crossley Tender bellowed into view, they were ready. Thomas squinted through the raised rifle sights and grunted in satisfaction. Christ, there must be eighteen or twenty of 'em. His sight swung back and rested on the Tan, swaying near the tailboard, rifle between his knees, hands clenched around the butt. As Thomas steadied himself, gun and arms resting on top of the bank, the Tan suddenly raised his right hand and removing his cap, he ran a finger inside the rim, before turning slightly to the fat soldier sitting beside him.

Above on the rise, the sun climbed higher. Thomas closed one eye, scanned along the sights of the Lee Enfield and gently squeezed.

'THE LAUGHING BOY' WON THE 2011 CANON SHEEHAN SHORT STORY AWARD AT DONERAILE ARTS FESTIVAL.

## Dreaming Dreams

She stands on the rocks, still as a statue. The soft breeze blows long strands of hair across her face. Only her eyes move, panning the harbour. Everything looks the same. The waves lazily caress the rocks out on the bay, spray rising like a fistful of confetti before falling and disappearing back into the sea again. The house still stands on the headland, defiant, like an old crone with something to prove.

Twenty years ago, it had been like that too. They'd walked here, laughed, dreamed. 'We'll buy it!' The woman's voice, light, seductive, slips round in her head. She hears it as clearly as if it were yesterday. 'And every evening, we'll look out towards the lighthouse and think of the long ago ships and the sailors and the swell of the sea. And we'll pull closer to the fire, safe and warm, and the days and nights will slip quietly past but we won't mind because we'll be together.'

Poetic almost, her words had been.

Now, she allows herself a faint smile, so faint it is more a slight lifting of her lips, as she returns to the present. The soft insidious whisper in her head fading. Behind her is the village with its long straggling street and the three storied building at the end, ugly, unpainted, facing towards the harbour, empty for as long as she can remember. The voice rises again, persuasive, licking around the outside of her memory, echoing- 'perfect for a hostel. We could do it. Think of all the hikers passing through and nowhere for them to stay? It would be perfect, perfect.' The voice fades again as a swarm of gulls swoop out of nowhere, cackling furiously, drowning out the soft, feminine voice in her head...

The tiny cage stands empty. The stream of sunlight through the window arches towards the corner of the room, showing up the dust, the cobwebs. Both of them, on hands and knees, searching, calling, under the table, behind bookshelves, the steps of the open back door, until finally cornered. Tiny nose darting and eyes filled with terror at the accidental bid for freedom, until the voice soothes it and its tiny heartbeat slows and the tiny creature stops trembling long enough to be picked up and safely cuddled, fur smooth against her neck. Her eyes meet the woman's and they laugh, weak with relief that the creature is safe, not lost forever among the rocks in the garden, at the mercy of predators.

Taking a deep breath now, she closes her eyes. She's forgotten the smell. That salty, damp tang, like nothing else she's ever breathed anywhere. It caresses her face as she climbs the narrow road, hedgerows lush with exuberant, orange montbretia, the red bells of the fuchsia tolling soundlessly in the breeze. And then cresting the rise, there it is, the sea, stretching away, away, beyond the horizon. And she is breathless, not because of the climb, but at the sheer beauty of that vast expanse of blue - inviting, sparkling, magical. And the whisper of the woman curls itself around her mind saying how beautiful it is, the whisper itself a caress, warm breath soft against her skin- 'this is heaven and we're there already.' And the soft gurgle, the feel of the woman's hand and the expression on her face as she looks at her.

And the midnight walks, the muffled, lazy sound of the waves just beyond the roadside fields, the moon and the flicker of the lights of the far away lighthouse, together casting a long ladder of light over the countryside. A strange, almost hypnotic calm enveloping the winding road into the village, stealing into their very bones, wrapping itself around them until there existed only that moment in that place - there was no past, no future, only the present - and the two of them. There was no traffic, only their footfall to break the silence of the night. The soft whinnying of the horse, head over the old rusting gate, was like an explosion in the stillness so that they started, before laughing at their foolishness. The moonlight dappled lightly over the hundreds of wild garlic growing on the hedgerows, the scent filling their nostrils, so that the silence and the faint swishing of the waves, the gently weaving trees and the odour of the garlic, so seduced her senses that she was almost giddy, heady with the perfection of that moment and that place - and the woman.

Twenty years ago.

She moves slightly on the rocks. Behind her, the village has retreated into the twilight, the houses huddling together, holding each other up almost, as they have done for centuries in the face of storms and gales and time.

She nods slowly, yes, time, above all, time.

She is motionless, staring unseeingly out at the lighthouse. Its beam sweeping the countryside, boldly, brightly. It picks her out for a moment, pinpointing her in its unchanging light, before dismissing her and moving on, leaving her in the twilight, almost invisible now among the grey shadows.

## Isaac's Farmhouse

Hurrying along the narrow country road, Jean cursed herself for not bringing an umbrella, though when she'd left home, the sun had been shining brightly. But now, she glanced upwards, a mass of heavy grey clouds, scudded across the sky. How could she have forgotten the whims and fancies of the Irish weather, she scolded herself? The telegraph poles growled and the branches of the beech trees lining the sides of the road, lurched and swayed, reminding her of the young woman she'd seen last winter in Kensington High Street, wrestling with a large golf umbrella, which had turned itself inside out in the gale. She smiled a little at the picture in her mind.

She soon stopped smiling, realizing that there was going to be the mother of all thunder showers and unless she found herself some shelter rapidly, she'd be soaked to the skin in her light coat, cotton trousers and totally unsuitable canvas walking shoes. She couldn't believe how fast the wind had risen. A heavy crash of thunder nearby forced her to concentrate. She looked at the swaying trees at either side of her. She had to get away from them. Worse place to be in a thunder storm. She remembered what happened to Paddy Bowles from the village years ago and shuddered. Her mother had used the example of poor Paddy for years to frighten herself and her brothers from ever taking shelter under any kind of tree in a storm. No, forget the trees. So what was she to do? Think, woman, think, she told herself as she pushed the hair out of her eyes and tried to keep her balance against the rushing wind.

She stopped for a moment in the middle of the road and looked around her, getting her bearings. She nodded. Yes, she was right. Isaacs' old farmhouse wasn't far away. She hadn't really thought about the place for years. It had been derelict for decades, having fallen into wrack and ruin since the death of Mr. Samuel oh, it must be all of twenty- five years ago now, definitely well before she left for London. But, she told herself, any port in a storm. She hurried along for a couple of hundred metres before turning off the main road and into the small laneway leading to the farmhouse - just in time, as there was an enormous growl of thunder, quickly followed by another and then the rain came, almost blinding her. Hurry, hurry, she told herself as she half ran, half stumbled across the empty yard, fat drops striking her face, as she fumbled, hands slippery with moisture, at the unlocked front door, before falling into the silence of the narrow hallway beyond.

She let out a long loud breath. Phew, that was close. She shook her hair out vigorously before taking off her coat and shaking that out too. Here, the sound of raindrops was fainter and though she could still hear the thrumming of the wind through the chimney, it, too, was fainter and softer somehow. Jean remembered her grandfather, when she was just a small girl, saying the older houses in the parish like the Isaacs, the O' Donnells, the Kellehers and their own old farmhouse, were built to withstand all kinds of weather. 'Ah, they knew how to build in them days,' he used to say with satisfaction as the gales whirled around outside and they sat snug and safe around the large open fire in their own big farmhouse, large flames crackling and leaping upwards in the huge grate.

Now that she was here and would be for some time, more than likely, she might as well explore the old place, give her something to do. She'd start with the room on her left, the one nearest to her, just inside the door. It was a large room, probably once the sitting room. She glanced around and shivered slightly. There was something lost and lonely about empty houses. The grate of the large fireplace running halfway along one wall was piled high with small twigs, which spilled carelessly out onto the bare floor. Evidence of years of nest building, she thought. Further down the narrow corridor was the kitchen, faded green cupboards hung drunkenly from the walls and an old water jug, snug in a blanket of cobwebs, stood on a dust-covered timber table.

It was the same throughout the house – old newspapers in the corner of a bedroom, frames of beds rotting peacefully away into dust, a man and woman dressed in clothes popular more than half a century before, stared out severely from a dusty picture frame. Jean wondered who they were. She bent and examined their faces. No, she had never seen them so they must have lived here well before her time. Maybe Mr. Samuel's parents? Jean felt sad to think how vibrant busy lives were reduced to this - lifeless mementoes covered in dust and cobwebs. People had lived their whole lives here, struggled in hard times, celebrated their triumphs - dying here too, peacefully in their beds after a lifetime of working the land. Looking around, she imagined the memories of decades absorbed into the stone of the walls, embedded there.

Back in the kitchen again, she went through yet another doorway, door dangling from rotting hinges. Stepping gingerly through, she came out into what appeared to be a small scullery - then stopped dead on the threshold. There, in front of her, just to the right of the door was a large old bookcase, the wood dark and dusty, punctured with tiny holes. It was squeezed in between the listing door and the little window criss-crossed with cobwebs and grime. Jean didn't see the grime and the dust, what made her eyes open in astonishment were the lines of old books, strewn higgeldy, piggeldy across its shelves. Fugitives from a ruthless house clearance sometime in the not so recent past, by the looks of it. Jean looked at the volumes. Filling the top shelf was a complete set of *Dickens* in yellows and blues and greens, *Little Dorrit, The Old Curiosity Shop, Oliver Twist, David Copperfield, Dombey and Son, Great Expectations*...In the shelf underneath, *Uncle Tom's Cabin* nestled up to a purple *Arabian Nights* while *Silas Marner* and *Northanger Abbey* snuggled together in the small space away over in the right hand corner. Jean reverently reached out an arm and turned back the dust cover of *Uncle Tom's Cabin*. On the flyleaf in beautiful clear copperplate she read, *'To Samuel Isaacs, for regular and punctual attendance, at Sunday School. From Rev. George Burrows. December 1912.'*

Jean remembered Mr. Samuel, from her younger days, a gentle old man with a silver topped walking cane and beautiful manners. How callous! As Jean reached for some of the books, they simply fell apart in her hands. Jean's lips tightened as a defeated *Vanity Fair* fluttered to the ground. Whoever was responsible for this sacrilege should be horse whipped. How could anyone consign these beautiful books to the damp and cold of a derelict shed? She tried to recall snippets of conversation she had picked up on her holidays home. Hadn't the GAA club bought the farm after Mr Samuel died and drawn up plans to develop the lands into playing pitches and a leisure centre or gym, or something like that? But of course, all those plans were made before the recession. Once that arrived, those fanciful notions had come to nought and nothing had been done in the years since. She frowned in concentration. Hadn't her brother mentioned that the house and the acre surrounding it were up for sale for years? But the price must have been too high, Jean guessed. At any rate, nobody was interested enough to buy.

But what kind of person could treat those beautiful books in such a way? Shame on them, Jean thought as she stared at the three sagging shelves holding their hundred- year old treasures, cobwebbed and colourful, magical and discarded. Glancing at the volumes again, Jean thought that their faded dust jackets held so many precious memories. What pleasure they must have given over the years to the old man, long since resting in the little Church of Ireland graveyard, just outside the village? She lost herself in images of the past- a little boy running home, proudly clutching his precious book. Had his mother, that severe figure in the photograph, smiled with pride as she tousled his hair and hugged him? Had they both caressed the cover and oohed and aahed over the beautiful illustrations, before the boy's father came in from the fields and his son ran eagerly towards him, holding his precious gift.

Jean shook herself and the picture disappeared. She was still for a moment, the quiet of the old place having lazily wrapped itself around her, enveloping her in a warm, unhurried embrace. She laughed and mocked herself for being fanciful. Then, she realized that the rain and wind seemed to have died down outside. She stood again looking at the lost books. She frowned, thinking furiously, gaze lingering on Wilkie Collins's *The Woman in White*. Then she made her decision. When she spoke, her own voice startled her in the silence.

'You, my friends,' she announced to the sleeping volumes, 'are about to be rescued. You're coming home with me. From now on, I promise you, you'll all be loved and useful again. What do you think of that?'

She paused as if waiting a reply from the silent bodies huddled together in the old bookcase, then nodded. 'Just you hang on there until I go and get my car.'

Her voice echoed through the dreaming rooms. She imagined she heard a deep contented sigh – Old Mr. Isaac's perhaps? Then rain and wind forgotten, she ran through the empty house, across the yard and out through the old sagging gate. She looked up at the grey sky and laughed aloud as a large raindrop plopped smartly onto her upturned face.

# The Cry of the Curlew

*April 2012*

    Emily sat at the kitchen table, oblivious of the patter of rain against the window and the roar of the Atlantic less than a quarter mile from the cottage. Eyes only on the white envelope, propped up between the milk jug and the sugar bowl in the centre of the table. She'd tossed and turned into the small hours, stomach churning, mind a cascading whirl of thoughts and half thoughts, and memories, above all, memories. Just after 4am, knowing she'd never sleep now, she'd thrown back the duvet and made her way to the kitchen, where she'd sat for the last hour cradling a mug of cold coffee, hands clenched around the mug, as memories tumbled into every corner of her mind.

    It was as if the last quarter of a century had never happened. She was a girl again, on the threshold of life, college beckoning and life was glorious, stretching endlessly and joyfully before her, full of promise and hope. But above all, full of love, love and passion for Hugh, Hugh Power, a farmer's son, from the other side of the village.

    Oh, Hugh, Hugh, she thought now, as the thin face, alight with humour flashed before her. Abruptly, she sprang to her feet, finding it difficult to breathe and frightened by the waves of panic washing over her. In her haste, she half stumbled against the table, arm catching the coffee mug which went spinning to the floor. She stood there, gasping, breath loud in the silence, supporting herself against the table, gazing at the yellow and blue shards strewn along the tiled floor. When her mouth opened, the cry was primitive, anguished, bouncing off the kitchen walls and ricocheting up from the tiled floor. Then, slumped against the kitchen wall, crying quietly now, she was unaware and uncaring even if she were, that the last faint flickers of darkness had disappeared from the sky and Friday April 18th was just beginning.

*The summer of 1987 in Clonmore had been a glorious one - day after day of blue skies and lazy sunshine. The river flowed languidly that last Sunday in July as Emily Bourke and Hugh Power wandered slowly along the bank at the bottom of the Nine Acre meadow, the one farthest away from the farmhouse, before climbing up leisurely to the top of the field, where there was a glorious view out over the surrounding countryside - a view that took in three counties.*

*It was Hugh's farm now, too, or it would be one day when his father retired. She stole sideways looks at him and marvelled at how handsome he was. Since he'd left school in June, he'd worked full time alongside his father. He'd filled out too, he was no longer the schoolboy she'd known all her life but a man, doing a man's job on the farm and working like his father and old Tim Connors, the farm labourer, late into the night. But Hugh loved every square inch of the land, the cattle, the early mornings and late nights. 'I could never work in an office,' he'd told her earnestly,' shure, I'd stifle, even the thought of it...' he'd shuddered.*

*Hand in hand, they'd ambled along that afternoon, making plans for the future they'd share after Emily got her degree. Suddenly, Hugh pulled her by the hand and half ran, half dragged her up the last few yards to the top of the hill.*

*'Shush, listen.'*

*Then she heard it, a loud cry travelling upwards from the river. Plaintive, drawn-out, haunting. A cry that would bring tears to the eyes.*

*She turned.*

*Hugh's eyes were bright, dancing with excitement.*

*'It's a curlew,' he answered her unspoken question. 'Isn't it beautiful, it's the bird of the high grass and the marshlands.'*

*He gripped her hand.*

*'We are so lucky to hear it; the curlew is really shy – a bit like you are at times.'*

*Emily laughed.*

*'But, look, look down, where the song is coming from.'*

*Dropping her hand, Hugh threw out his arms. Emily, trying to get her breath, gasped at the magnificent view down the valley. They could see for miles. Below them, the river, sparkling in the sunlight, winding its way lazily through the large meadow, separating Power's farm from Grogan's land and beyond, the distant mountains a blue haze in the stillness of the summer's evening. They were both silent for a moment.*

*'I feel like we're on top of the world,' Emily said dreamily, looking at the countryside rolling away before them, 'like God must feel looking down on the world,' she laughed and then jigging up and down, hugged Hugh impulsively and catching both his hands danced him round and round, singing 'We're on the top of the world...'*

*Exhausted and laughing, they both fell to the ground and then Hugh turned. 'I've been thinking,' he began, 'wouldn't this be a wonderful spot for our house? I would get the curlew to serenade you every morning.' Laughing, he'd pushed her down on the grass and sat beside her, arms around her shoulders. Emily felt the tears in her eyes and wondered she didn't explode with happiness and love.*

*'Don't move, please, don't move.'*

*Suddenly serious, he'd looked her straight in the eye, startling her. 'I have to tell you, Miss Emily Bourke, that you're now sitting in the living-room of the Power house with your feet on a plush rug that has been bought at enormous expense, and shipped all the way from Persia, especially for you, and please, please be careful that your sandals don't mess ...'*

'*Idiot,*' *she'd pummelled him playfully and as he caught her arms, he rolled her over and over until she couldn't get her breath. She looked up at him laughing and then stopped, as his head came down, shutting out the sunlight. She felt his lips on hers and after that, she had no conscious thought anymore.*

*At first, she'd not thought anything wrong, just felt she was a bit under the weather. It was only on the last Friday in September, two weeks before college began, that Emily finally admitted to herself that she was pregnant. She was shocked and terrified. Numb, incapable of thought, she sat, frozen on the bed, despite the warm sun spilling lazily through the open window. What would her parents say, their only child, the child they had such hopes for, college, a degree, independence-all the things denied to them in their day, because they couldn't afford them. When she thought of all their sacrifices, their disappointment, the terror threatened to overwhelm her. Jumping up from the bed, she grabbed her cardigan and rushed through the kitchen, ignoring her mother's call and grabbing her bicycle from the old shed, pedalled furiously down the lane in the direction of Powers' farm, only one thought racing around her head, like a merry go round, faster and faster. Hugh, Hugh, I must see Hugh, I must tell him, he'll know what to do, he'll know, he'll know.*

*He was working in the far field when she arrived. She could see him on the tractor as she cycled up the lane. Hurrying across the yard, she was grateful there was no sign of Irene, Hugh's mother, waving from the kitchen window, insisting she come in for a cup of tea. She didn't have to worry about Peter, his father. Being Friday, she knew he'd be away at the mart in Blackwater and wouldn't be* back until late evening. Hugh didn't notice her at first, so she watched the tractor until it turned at the corner of the field, her hands clenching and unclenching. Then, he saw her and the tractor stopped. As he jumped down, she saw his face light up and he waved as he hurried across the field. As he came closer, she saw that his face was anxious and he was frowning.

'Emily,' he stopped a few feet away from her, 'Is there something wrong?' She'd nodded mutely and he closed the last few yards between them and put his arms around her. Taking a deep breath, she'd pushed him away and looking up into his face, she blurted out the words, the first time she'd said them aloud to anyone.

'I'm pregnant,' voice quivering in spite of herself.

His face didn't change and for a moment, he'd said nothing so that she felt the fear rising again, knotting, twisting in her stomach.

'Oh Emily,'

Putting out his hand, he'd gently touched her face. To her amazement, he was smiling. She felt faint with relief.

'Pregnant oh, Emily', he'd said again. Then, catching her hands, he'd pulled her towards him. 'A baby, oh, Emily, our baby,'

Abruptly, he stopped. 'Oh, heavens, what am I thinking of - the baby.'

Gently patting her flat stomach, he'd led her to the hedge and sat her down on the grass, carefully as if she were china, the untidy mop of black curls flopping. He looked so ridiculous, she'd burst out laughing, all her fears evaporated and she felt a peace steal over her.

'Oh, God, Emily,' he'd whispered in her ear, 'When I saw your face, I thought you'd come to tell me you were breaking up with me.'

He pulled her close, holding her fiercely. 'We'll be alright. You can still get your degree,' he'd promised her, 'it will just be a bit later than we'd planned, that's all.'

She'd drawn a shaky breath-how could she have doubted him?

Before she left, they'd arranged to tell both sets of parents on the following Sunday afternoon. He'd insisted on walking her down the lane, pushing her bike with one hand and holding her hand with the other. He was full of happiness, choosing one name after another before discarding each one in favour of yet another new one. It was with great difficulty that she'd dissuaded him from accompanying her the whole three miles home. He wondered anxiously if she should be cycling at all in her condition. She'd laughed, but gently so as not to hurt his feelings. She felt suddenly so protective of him and refusing to allow him come further, kissed him on the cheek and left him standing at the end of the lane, still with that faint worried look on his thin face. 'Be careful, Emily,' he'd warned her 'Don't do anything that might harm yourself or our baby,' He'd smiled then. 'Imagine, our baby.'

He'd given her one last hug and when she'd reached the bend in the road, she'd turned and blown him a kiss. As she cycled home, she laughed aloud, she could hardly believe herself to be the same person who'd set out so full of terror, only an hour or so before.

It was a freak accident. Everyone said so. Old Tim Connors, who'd worked at Powers all his life repeated the same words, like a mantra, to anyone that would listen. When he'd climbed onto the tractor, Hugh had been standing well to the side of the trailer. 'Do *ye think I'd have driven off if there was any danger to the lad?'* he'd asked over and over again.

*No one blamed Tim. How could they? Whatever possessed Hugh to suddenly dash between the tractor and trailer, no one would ever know now. When Tim had stumbled from the cab and knelt by the prone figure lying on the ground, he had time only to murmur an Act of Contrition in Hugh's ear before he was gone.*

*Emily lay in bed for weeks, unaware of what was going on. She didn't attend Hugh's funeral, didn't even realise it had taken place. She was beside herself, her mother and father, were frantic and helpless in the face of such anguish. It was Christmas before she'd begun to resemble anything like herself again.*

*The Powers never knew of Hugh's baby. What was the point, her father had asked, reasonably? 'By giving the child up for adoption, you'll be giving it the best chance it can have in life.'*

*'Shure, aren't you only a child yourself,' her mother said, 'How can you bring up a baby, it wouldn't be fair on you or the child and you, with all your life in front of you.'*

After graduation, she'd got a job in Galway and rented a small cottage beside the sea just out beyond Clifden. Of the child, the little boy, she rarely thought, she couldn't, resolutely shutting him away in the deepest recesses of her mind. She'd managed successfully for over a quarter of a century- until the arrival of the letter. At first, she'd ignored that too, until the early hours of that awful morning, sitting at the table when she'd wept for Hugh and the young girl she'd been, and above all, for the baby she'd given away, their baby. When she stopped crying, she'd felt calmer and she'd read the letter again. Long before she came to the end, she felt the yearning. She knew then she'd answer the letter.

Emily stopped for a moment outside the *Imperial Hotel*. Hands shaking, she took a deep breath and then she was through the revolving doors. At first, she could see nothing, blinded by the brightness of the early morning sun outside. But quickly, her eyes grew accustomed to the dimness and she looked around, biting her lip. At first, she thought he hadn't come and she felt her legs go weak with disappointment, despair even. But then, she saw the figure struggle from the armchair by the window. And he was there in front of her, standing hesitantly, a mop of untidy dark hair falling over his forehead. Her heart gave a great lurch as the past and the present merged for a moment and she was dizzy- but only for a moment.

And then, she felt a great calm and moved forward, hands outstretched, to greet him.

# Sonny

It was glorious. The sun was sparkling. That's what jewels must look like, Sonny thought, then laughed, realising that the sparkling sun on the iron roofs of the cowshed was probably the nearest thing a fella like him would come to seeing a jewel. He looked around the lane as he drove the cattle back into their pasture, marvelling at the beauty of nature around him. One of the fields he passed belonged to Mattie Roche and was full of daffodils, a blanket of yellow, swaying gently in the early morning breeze.

Mattie was elderly, nearly blind and his farming days were over. But in his heyday, as he was fond of telling everyone, he could puck a ball with the best of them. And he was the best man in the parish behind a plough. Sonny could well believe it, even at 88, Mattie was still a huge man with hands as big and wide as shovels and a voice that could be heard two fields away. What a pity, Sonny though sadly, he couldn't see the beauty around him.

Thinking that, he became immersed in his own thoughts for a moment. He thought about old age and how awful it must be. Not being able to do things for yourself anymore, depending on people to drop in to see to your needs. Worst of all though, must be not able to see. Sonny had excellent eyesight, he looked around at the hedgerows, the bird on the tree a few yards away and shuddered. He couldn't imagine not being able to see. Surrounded all the time by thick blackness.

I'd hate to be old, he thought. He went once with his mother, when she called to deliver some messages from the shop in the village. He felt like bolting when he went into the dark little house. He could hardly get his breath and he stayed there, rigid, without moving, until his mother was finished and they said goodbye to the old man. Even now, he shivered just thinking about it.

His attention was brought back to the present when he noticed that the cows had stopped and were lazily chewing grass at the side of the lane. 'Hup there,' he raised his voice, waving his arms and stick while he ran from one side of the narrow lane to the other to get the herd moving again. Slowly, as if resenting having to leave the juicy grass at the roadside, they moved off reluctantly, tails swishing indignantly, still chewing. Up to a few months ago, he had Robin, the sheepdog, best they ever had, his father said. Sonny had never remembered the farmyard without Robin. But old age too, had caught up with him and Robin was buried now down in the orchard under the biggest and oldest tree there. There had been tears a plenty. Sonny thought it was hard to say goodbye to anyone you loved, a dog was no different.

They'd reached the field and Sonny went ahead to open the wooden gate. And then, well used to the routine, the cows ambled through the gap at their own slow pace. Sonny followed, closing the gate firmly behind him and guiding the cows into the next pasture.

He was almost at the centre of the field when suddenly the peace of the morning was shattered by a loud report. Sonny stood there transfixed for a moment. What was going on? The report echoed again and again and the cows began to run ungainly all over the field. Then Sonny came alive- it was gunshots, his eyes wildly swung away from the field and across the small river to the height of the road leading into the village. So great was his shock that he couldn't focus at first and his heart first nearly stopped beating altogether and then began to beat so rapidly and so loudly, he thought it would choke him.

Tans, a lorry load of them. One was standing at the back of the Crossley Tender and waving a gun around and then shooting to the great amusement of his friends who were swarming around the lorry. Sonny could hear their laughter quite plainly. He stood still with terror for a moment, unaware that he was emitting small whimpering cries and his hand was opening and closing almost of its own accord. He knew the reputation of the Tans – murdering bastards, his father, not a swearing man, had called them. Why only last week, they had shot and wounded poor Maggie Kelleher for the sheer hell of it. She'd been walking to the village and a lorry load of Tans had trundled past. The poor woman hadn't been quick enough to get out of their way. It was too late when she heard them and they'd simply shot at her as they passed and passed on screaming with drunken laughter. Target practice they'd called it for the IRA scumbags they were going to destroy. Now their laughter, raucous and coarse wafted across the distance between them. Sick with terror, he was immune to the yellow stream of water trickling down his legs inside the heavy pants. With a low groan, forgetting about the panicked cows, he stumbled across the field towards the gate, intent only on reaching home safely. 'Father,' he called weakly as he stumbled along 'Father, Father,'

Meanwhile, in the farmhouse, Brendan and Kate heard the shots coming from the Height. They looked at each other briefly. There was only one thought in their heads - Sonny. Brendan raced as fast as his shaking legs would take him down the lane, all the time praying to every saint he could think of. Sonny would panic, he'd never take shelter and lay low on the ground where he'd be safe. He was little more than a child and he was out there among the gunfire. As Brendan was almost half-way down the boreen, the gunfire stopped. The silence increased his terror.

'Sonny, he called frantically, 'Sonny lad, where are you?'

Reaching the gate, he opened it, breathlessly. Looking around he could only see the panicked cows, like some vast ungainly prehistoric creatures, running aimlessly, their pink udders swinging to and fro like mad things. Of Sonny himself, there was no sign. Brendan stopped for a moment to get his breath and then half ran, half stumbled across the field, the cows opening out and scattering before him. It was then he saw him - face down on the ground, no movement 'Ah Jesus, no, no,' Brendan was scarcely aware he was speaking. He threw himself beside his son and was about to turn him over when he saw the gaping wound in his back. When Kate arrived beside him, Brendan was bent low on the ground, head close to that of his still son, whispering. She sank to her knees and almost instinctively, joined in.

'Oh my God, I am heartily sorry...'

In Mattie Roche's field, the daffodils swayed and danced in the early morning breeze.

# Sanctuary

*In Nomine Patris et Filis, et Spiritu u Sanctus...*

He stood at the back of the cathedral, slightly hidden behind the pillar, head buzzing, barely registering the entrance of the priest. Wrapped around his throat was a thickly knitted muffler and there was a screen of dust on his brown leather boots.

He had one chance and one only, he knew that. It had to happen between the cathedral porch and the street, a distance of only four hundred yards or so. If the bastard made it to the street, he'd be protected by his bodyguards and the chance would be lost. The young man frowned and bit his lip. His feet, in their brown boots with the scuffed toecaps, moved restlessly on the stone floor. He tried to shut out his jumbling thoughts, his worry and fear about the many things that could go wrong. The what ifs? There were so many what ifs that he'd be completely paralysed, and do nothing at all if he gave too much thought to them all.

Success depended on the cathedral being crowded. The 11am Mass was always thronged, they'd assured him. He looked around anxiously, he wondered if that was true, he couldn't quite see from here. The pillar was in his way and he didn't want to draw any attention to himself by advancing further into the cathedral. What if they were wrong? He expelled a slow breath, conscious of the silent worshippers in the pews near him and told himself to calm down. You wouldn't know who among the worshippers could be trusted. Even now, there could be someone in one of the pews eyeing him up and noting that he was a stranger. He looked at them but they were all praying, heads bowed, some twisting rosary beads between their fingers. He could feel the cold sweat on his forehead.

He wasn't worried about his own fate, didn't even think of it. Death no longer held any terror for him. In the last eight months, he'd become immune to it. He'd seen too much, diced with it so often, meted it out until he'd lost count of how many he'd killed. He remembered his own men, young like himself, all of them, and his face hardened. Young Jamie barely nineteen, dying in a ditch with a bullet through the head in the Gleann na gCapall ambush in May, Morgan and Tommy cut down in a raid on the Tullybawn police barracks the following month. His own Flying Column barely escaping from McCarthy's safe house only three weeks before.

*Oremus...*

He smiled humorlessly, as he watched the priest raise the chalice on the altar. Were it not for young Fenton's bladder, they'd never have heard the Tans approach and would have been caught like rats in a trap, just like the Curramore ambush back in August when the bastards surrounded an old farmhouse and murdered twelve volunteers in cold blood. His face darkened at the memory. His column should have learned from that – they'd been careless at McCarthys and were lucky to get away over the hills, the Tans so close behind them, they could almost feel the hot breath on their necks. But they were country boys, all of them, and knew the terrain like the back of their hands. That's what saved them that night, that and their desperation.

He pulled his attention back from the frantic flight over rough terrain, in the darkness, and concentrated on what was going on around him. Narrowing his eyes, he watched as queues of worshippers made their way to the altar rails and knelt, heads bowed while Monsignor O' Brien worked his way along the lines, murmuring. He couldn't hear the words from where he stood, he didn't have to, he knew exactly what O'Brien was saying, 'Corpus Christi, Corpus Christi.' It was a long time since he was at the altar rails but like all Catholic boys and girls, the words of the Mass were trapped deep inside his soul.

The Monsignor was passionately anti- IRA, they'd told him. He knew a few himself like the Monsignor, precious little understanding or sympathy in their big parochial houses, fat cats, afraid to rock the boat in case they lost their privileges in a new Ireland. Thank God though that all the clergy wasn't like that, there were many priests and nuns who understood and supported their vision of a free nation and helped them out in any way they could.

*Deus, qui nobis sub sacramento...*

His mind turned back to the present. Brown, Samuel Brown of the Royal Irish Constabulory. Stationed in Clonmore for only eight months, yet in that time he had proved himself a thorough bastard. What made it worse was that he was an Irishman, a Catholic, from Mayo and this made his brutality harder to stomach than the sadism of the Tans and Auxiliaries.

Browne hated the IRA, 'murdering thugs', he called them and collaborated in every way he could with the Tans. He'd been given a number of warnings but refused to listen to any of them. So the decision was made. Not only was Brown an Irishman and what he was doing stuck in the craw, but his assassination would also act as a warning to other members of the RIC, making them rethink their position in the force. If they could frighten enough of them to leave, it would make it very difficult, even impossible, for the British to rule the country effectively.

Brown though, was a cautious man and so far, this caution had kept him safe. Every time he appeared in public, he was accompanied by an armed escort. Yet, this same man, cautious as he was, refused to let his military escort accompany him inside the gates of the cathedral, insisting on walking the 400 yards or so from the public street to St. Oliver's on his own. Did a ruthless bastard like Browne actually believe that he was safe on church soil, that nobody would touch him, dare touch him, on sacred ground? Whatever Browne's reasons for walking unarmed and unaccompanied to weekly Mass, arrogance or innocence, the young man in the shadow of the pillar in the church porch was grateful for it.

*Glorie Patri et filio et spiritui sancto*

He tensed as the Monsignor prepared to bestow the final blessing. Quietly, he slipped from beside the pillar and made his way through the porch, out into the hard autumn sunlight and waited, leaning against the cathedral wall, then bending to fiddle with the bicycle clip on his trouser leg, to avoid notice by the few elderly men leaving the church porch early. His hands tightened as the crowds emerged laughing, talking, packed tightly together. But where was the bastard? He straightened, eyes darting from side to side, heart racing. He was nowhere to be seen. He swore silently.

Then he expelled a deep breath and felt his heart slowing slightly as he saw him in the middle of the throng, hatless, tall. Quickly, casually, he slipped into the middle of the worshippers, mingling with them and manoeuvring his way through the bodies to get close to Brown. Everything else faded. Easy now, easy. One, two, three steps. He was now directly behind him. Less than one hundred yards to go to the street.

Now, now, it had to be now!

Without taking his hand from his coat pocket, he fired three shots in rapid succession and kept walking. Before he swerved sideways, he saw Browne stumble, then fall. In the confusion, the shouting, and screaming of people scrambling across the church yard to the steps to get out onto the safety of the street, no one knew where the shots came from. In the mayhem, the young man allowed himself to be carried along to the street by the fleeing, panic-stricken mob.

No one noticed him. Why would they - in his worn jacket and scuffed boots, he was just one more country boy attending Mass where RIC Inspector Samuel Browne was shot by an unknown assailant or assailants. No one saw anything, they all swore to that afterwards. The bodyguards racing up the steps from the street after the gunfire saw nothing either. They were too intent for the first few minutes in checking if Brown were dead or alive to have the presence of mind to think of who might have shot him. By the time they regained their senses and realised that someone among the couple of hundred worshippers had to have been an IRA assassin, it was too late, far too late. The young man was already pedalling away down the small country by-road out of town, his gun thrown into the ditch beside Nugent's farm gate where it would be picked up later by a comrade.

By nightfall, it was all over the county that Inspector Samuel Brown of the RIC had been assassinated on his way out of Mass by the IRA. By that time, however, the young man had re-joined his column over twenty- five miles away to the west, ready for the next act of defiance against His Majesty's forces in Ireland.

# Waiting

She hates the darkness, fears it. She makes a sound now, not sure whether it's a sob or a laugh. She stifles it as she feels the small, damp hand twitch in hers, steadying herself with a deep breath, then another. She must not lose control. But she is suffocating. The air is fetid, pressing against her, smothering. Her body is covered with perspiration and her bones ache. She caresses the hand on her lap and turning sideways, bends and brushes her lips against the soft cheek.

How long have they been here? Hours, days? She shifts slightly and the hand tightens in hers. There has been no sound for a long time, not even the scampering of rats or mice, or whatever the creatures are that they share the darkness with. She shudders and closes her eyes.

The village had been a somersault of panic and dread for months. The people waiting and the sun shining. The days and nights passing in a slow tumble of light and shadow and heat and shade. Rumours scrambling over each other like living things, each one more terrifying than the last. The villagers sweltering in unbearable heat as each day passed and still nothing happened. But they lived with the terror: – waking, eating, sleeping, working, pushing the perspiration from their eyes and staring at the empty dirt road leading to the distant north.

At last it came, as they had known it would. She was feeding rice to the child when she heard it. At first, she thought herself mistaken, deceived by months of imaginings and false alarms and she stopped, spoon halfway to the child's mouth. But no, there it was again, a series of booms like muffled drums, coming from the dirt road, an indolent serpent winding itself back all the way to the city several days' trek away.

The child's eyes widened, the pupils darting sideways, but made no sound. Strangely, for a long moment, there was no sound anywhere. It was as if the village had been sucked into the very atmosphere itself, giving it the chance to take a last collective breath before being spat out, defenceless, puny, against the approaching madness.

From outside the open window, voices, an avalanche of voices, shrill, rapid, urgent. In the room, she could smell it, the terror, the helplessness, the inevitability, and as she laid the rice on the blood red tongue of the child, her hand trembled.

Now she prays for courage, but fears her God is far away, powerless to help them. Has abandoned them, even. She pushes the thought aside but it lingers, like a mist coiling itself into her mind, settling there, taunting, laughing.

She feels the child move beside her and clamber onto her lap. She strokes the hair, damp, smelling of stale sweat and begins to croon softly. It is a rhyme her mother used to chant to her as they played games in the wood when she was very young. Shouts of laughter, rising in rhythm with the words as she clasped her mother's hand, trotting along on small legs.

*It's a long way to Tipperary,*

*It's a long way to go*

*It's a long way to Tipperary*

*To the sweetest girl I know...*

Thousands of miles and a wide ocean ago ...

Her eyes jerk open. The child stiffens on her lap but remains silent. She hears a door burst open somewhere on the corridor outside, volleys of shouts, marching feet and a storm of voices, high pitched, alien. She swallows and puts the child gently from her, forcing her body upright. Her legs are shaky and she staggers, praying that she won't fall, that she will be strong. She reaches for the child's hands, gripping them. Against her, she feels the small body trembling.

The knob turns, roughly, uselessly. The strange voices, high, excited, a crash against the door. It doesn't budge. Then, more shouts and grunts, the door judders but still holds. It is only a matter of seconds though, she knows that. She pulls the child closer. The wood is splintering now, creaking like an old arthritic knee joint. Not long now, not long.

Her lips move above the child's head and the words come softly...

*It's a long way to Tipperary,*

*It's a long way to go*

*It's a long way to Tipperary*

*To the sweetest girl I know...*

## Miners' Alley

He'd watched her for months. Every Friday night, she and her friends at the bar in *Kavanagh's Hotel*. All in their twenties, drinking too much, laughing too loudly and spending too freely. There were usually six or seven of them, but it was the dark- haired one who caught his eye. Flamboyant, loud, scantily dressed like all the rest of them. There was just something about her though that made her stand out from the others, he didn't know what and didn't really care. He just knew she was the one. He didn't, couldn't, take his eye off her. The others may not as well be there for all the attention he showed them. But he was careful. He made sure she didn't notice him, that none of them noticed him. He was good at merging into the shadows. So he sat there alone, under the faded photograph of the *Clonroe Intermediate hurling champions 1997*, nursing his pint, brooding and watching, always watching.

The cool air hit him, fresh invigorating. Coat collar pulled up, he walked rapidly away from the hotel. A big man, well over 6 feet but trim and fit, not an ounce of excess weight, long strides, never hesitating. After a few minutes, he turned off the main street abruptly and plunged down a side street. He continued walking as the street narrowed, only slowing when he reached a dark narrow laneway – Miners' Alley, a short cut between the Market Square and the street leading to the estate of houses at the rear of George's Street, beside the canal.

His feet made no sound as he hurried down the narrow alleyway. He knew this area like the back of his hand. Knew every inch of the town he'd been living in for the last ten years. He knew too that the chances of meeting anyone else in the alley at this time of night were slim. He'd walked it countless times in the last few months at this hour and rarely met anyone. He'd watched the alley from the inside of the old store for hours. There was little risk and even if there was, it added to his excitement, made his breath come quicker. Tonight though, all was quiet, but for the faint echoes of cars from the direction of the town centre. By the time he reached the middle of the alleyway, he hadn't met a soul. He grinned tightly. God, he was one lucky bastard.

Half way down, he stopped beside a tall high building and looked up and down the alley. The door of *Hanleys' Grainstore*, was unlocked. Derelict now, falling down almost, never used anymore. He'd checked. He always checked everything. It paid to be careful, that way you didn't make mistakes. He had no intention of being caught now. After all, he'd got away with the others, the guards not even coming close. No, he was one lucky bastard alright. Reaching the doorway, he looked around quickly, sharply before stepping inside. All he had to do now was wait in the dimness and listen for the sounds coming down the laneway. The inside of the building was as familiar to him as his shed at home. It should be, he thought, after all the hours he'd spend there, watching, observing, over the last few months.

It was beginning to rain lightly now but it wouldn't matter. Slipping his hands deep into his pockets he pulled out a pair of rubber gloves and a mask – a *Mickey Mouse* mask. He grinned again, the irony of using a cartoon figure appealed to him. Before slipping on the gloves, he quickly removed the ring from his left hand and slipped it into his pocket. He pulled on the gloves, his breathing quickening. He looked at his watch. Almost time now. Almost time.

She was making such a racket with those ridiculous high heels that she wouldn't have heard a truck, he thought, as he watched her totter drunkenly down the alleyway. Her routine never varied, every Friday night was the same. Silly bitch, just like all the rest of them. All that watching for weeks in the pub, watching as she flirted and danced, skirt up to her arse and blouse so low, you could see her tits, well rounded, full firm. Wriggling and wheedling and driving men crazy. Unconsciously, he licked his lips. Asking for it, like all the others. Why dress like a tart otherwise? He remembered or thought he did, some judge up the country, making a similar comment and there had been the usual outcry from the bleeding hearts club. Fucking liberals, ruining the country. If his Emma dressed like that when she reached her teens, he'd take a whip to her and make no apologies for it.

Sluts, all of them, like that bitch teetering along the alley on her ridiculous heels. Drunk as well, he'd watched her, downing shorts like there was no tomorrow and shrieking with laughter with her friends. He grimaced with distaste. Stupid bitch, ignoring the warning from guards and the media not to walk alone in isolated places late at night. The clack of high heels on cobbles grew louder. He licked his lips again. He could feel the blood coursing through his veins. The adrenaline – oh God, the adrenaline, there was nothing on earth quite like it.

The woman knew nothing until he emerged silently from the doorway and came up behind her. She gave a yelp of terror and shock before the scream was cut off when he placed his hand firmly over her mouth. Weakly, she struggled but it was like the struggles of a dying bird. Roughly he pushed her through the door of the old grain store he'd left open behind him. She writhed and wriggled under his hands. Briefly he took his hand away from her mouth as he kicked the door shut. Before she could utter a sound though, he'd hit her with a backhander and her head swung back against one of the old wooden pillars and suddenly, she was still.

He whipped the clothes off her in a frenzy, breathing heavily. Short, quick breaths, grunting, sweating, images of her at the pub, flaunting, asking for it, flooded his mind. As he bent over her, he felt like a god, blood pumping, capable of anything. There was no one to stop him. No one! The knowledge was intoxicating and he laughed aloud, manically, like a man possessed.

Finally, he rolled back against the wall, gasping, sweating, the mist disappeared from in front of his eyes. He felt the rage flow out of him. He blinked and looked over at the girl. She lay there, unmoving.

Shit! He felt a sudden wave of panic. Had he hit her too hard? Christ, he hadn't killed her, had he? He leaned over and felt the pulse in her throat and almost sagged with relief. Yes, there was a pulse, faint but still there. Just knocked out, she'd be all right. Bitches like her always were. Wouldn't do much more flaunting, asking for it, in the future, that was for sure. From now on, she'd have a lot more respect for herself and act properly, with some degree of dignity. He nodded. Standing up, he staggered and held onto the wall, He stood still for a moment taking deep breaths before tearing the mask from his face and straightening his clothes. He felt quite calm now as he balled the gloves and mask together and thrust them deep into his trouser pockets. Then, giving the unconscious girl one last look, he turned, listened intently before slipping out into the darkness of the alley. Walking swiftly, he reached the busy Market Square in minutes and made his way to the car park at the top of Dominic Street.

By the time he'd showered, had a glass of brandy and eaten the dinner his wife Breda, had left ready for him, he felt better, more himself. Euphoric, filled with energy. He wished Breda hadn't taken the kids for an overnight with her mother. He'd have liked to talk, to feel the normality around him. Maybe have an early night, he grinned at the thought. Breda was a fine woman, respectable, all a woman should be.

The phone woke him. It was not yet fully light. As he reached out to pick it up, he squinted at the clock. 5.46am.

Yes,' he mumbled.

'Sorry Bill, to wake you so early, but we think he's struck again, the so called *Mickey Mouse* rapist, bloody sadist,'

It was the duty sergeant.

'Ah, Christ no, not again, where this time?

'Miners Alley, a warehouse, half way along the street, sometime last night.'

'Christ, where is she now, Did she see him?'

'Na, at the hospital, in a bad way. Could be looking at murder this time, hospital's not sure she'll pull through.'

He felt the ice somersault in his belly, brain razor sharp.

He sat up, wide awake now.

'What do you mean, not sure if she'll pull through?'

'Bastard knocked her about something terrible, would be dead for sure except one of the winos, using the warehouse to doss down, found her and raised the alarm. Poor sod, fit for hospital himself,'

'Be right there. Sick bloody bastard'.

His words were automatic. Worry gnawed his insides.

He was just about to cut the connection when he realised that the sergeant was still talking.

'Thing is, bastard slipped up this time. Found a wedding ring on the floor beside her.'

Detective Garda Bill Simons cradled the phone in his hand and gazed unseeingly at the mirror over the dressing table.

# The Witching Hour

It was just after midnight when Niall slipped out of the darkened house, shutting the back door with a soft click behind him. He paused, fingering the torch in his pocket, before plunging into the warren of narrow streets leading out of town.

The streets were almost deserted at this time of night and he met no one, except an elderly man, trailing a miserable little terrier behind him. Niall hurried along, keeping close to the darkness cast by the row of derelict houses on Dominick Street. Near St Michael's Church, he slid into the shadows and listened intently, hardly daring to breathe, but after a few minutes, wiped his hand across his forehead and slipped out again. There was no one following. Nerves, he told himself.

Resuming his rapid walk, he reached the outskirts of the town. Just beyond the last street-lamps, he slackened his pace slightly and switched on the small torch. The beam lit up the briars and bushes along the ditch, before suddenly falling on a five barred wooden gate. Jumping the gate easily, he ran across the field, oblivious of the damp grass soaking his runners and seeping into his socks.

In minutes, he was in the wood, walking along a narrow pathway bounded on each side by high beech trees. He walked confidently, now leaving one path and taking another, never pausing to see if he was going in the right direction. After about a quarter of an hour, he heard the sound of water in front of him. He nodded in satisfaction, before taking the left hand fork that ran parallel to the river. The air here was different – the wonderful aroma of the honeysuckle, made all the sweeter by the rain that had fallen earlier.

He smiled and his mind was filled with tumbling thoughts of long ago, when he was younger – an earlier and more innocent time.

He remembered Tom and himself mitching from school one gloriously sunny May morning. Deciding to play at being Tom Sawyer and Huckleberry Finn for the day, they'd filled their schoolbags with apples and biscuits and jam sandwiches - *Lambe's Jam,* full of juicy succulent strawberries. Even now remembering, he could almost feel the dripping of the juice down his chin as he bit into the sandwich.

They'd shoved their schoolbooks under Tom's bed, so that anyone coming into the room would have to hunker down on all fours before they could see them. They'd giggled at the idea of Mrs Connors, Tom's mother, hunkering down anywhere. The large rolls of fat that wobbled as she wheezed along made walking difficult enough, hunkering would be well-nigh impossible. Still laughing, they grabbed their bags and raced through the village, before taking this same path, whooping with glee, when they heard the bells of St Michael's chime 9 o clock.

'Poor suckers.' Tom had scoffed 'imagine, sweating inside doing sums on a day like this.'

What a glorious day it had been though, Niall thought now. They'd built a small fire in a circle of stones and roasted some potatoes they'd taken from Mickey Kelleher's ridges that morning. After they'd eaten, they'd both laid back, bellies full and watched as miles overhead, the sun danced and jiggled and played hide and seek among the tall branches, fanning out like a giant canopy above them. 'Ah, Jasus, if we died now,' Tom said dreamily,' we wouldn't have to go to heaven, shure, we're there already.'

Of course, they'd paid for their perfect day, clattered by their mothers when they'd straggled home hours later, tired and sunburnt and given extra homework and put in detention for the rest of the week by Master Hayes. You always did have to pay for your pleasure, Niall knew that now. He thought they knew it even then, but some things were worth the price you paid for them. You just had to know what was worth the punishment and what wasn't. Simple enough choices - most of the time.

The lightness in his face died away and he gnawed his lip. Hurrying along, the path becoming narrower now, more twisted and slippery. Were it not for the light of the torch, he would have had difficulty making out where he was. After a few minutes rapid walking, he left the path altogether and plunged into the thicket of trees, inching his way through the tangled undergrowth before eventually stepping out from the huge overhanging trees, into a small clearing.

He was breathing hard and there was a film of sweat on his forehead. Quickly, impatiently, he wiped it off. He looked at his watch, then switched off the torch before lowering himself down and settling himself against the trunk of an old tree. He began to bite his nails, then with a grimace of revulsion, picked up a small twig from the ground and began to chew, his left leg jiggling constantly. He looked around the clearing, but there was little he could see. Though the night was still cloudy, the moon was beginning to appear intermittently, its weak light lacing through the trees around him.

He laughed suddenly as he thought of Petie Flaherty, an old drunk in the village when he was growing up. He remembered Petie on the street, just outside his house one dark night as he tried to fumble his way home to the little cottage he shared with his brother, high on the hill above the village. Niall had cocked his head above the blankets as he listened admiringly to Petie's colourful language just on the other side of his bedroom window.

'Bad cess to you for a moon,' Petie had shouted, voice slurred 'bad cess to you again, I say, youse aul bastard, you'd be out alright on a bright night, b'jasus, you would so.'

Niall laughed again now, softly at the memory. If he hadn't heard it himself, he wouldn't have believed anyone would be thick enough to come out with a line like that. Ah, jay, you couldn't make up some things, he thought.

Of course Petie wasn't the only thick one, he thought, twiddling the twig around between his teeth, face becoming closed and pinched.

He stiffened, then springing to his feet, darted behind the tree trunk. His legs turned to jelly and waves of sweat broke out all over his body. Then he sagged as a short stocky figure appeared in the clearing before him.

'Stephen, Christ Almighty. You scared the bloody hell outa me, man.'

'Did you think you was gonna be eaten by the big bad wolf, lad? Stephen, thickset and middle aged, grinned and stepped a few paces back, squinting exaggeratedly, 'Janey, lad, you don't look much like little Red Riding Hood, that's for sure.'

Niall laughed uneasily.' I wasn't expecting you,' He expelled a long loud breath, letting the silence lengthen for a few moments

'Do you know what's up?'

'Nah,' the other man replied and flung himself on the ground' Just told turn up here after midnight and wait. Better be a bloody good reason,' he grumbled' ruining a bloody good Saturday night.' He wriggled into a more comfortable position.

'Maybe it's a stash,' Niall mused worriedly' although nothing's due for another while. Did he say nothing at all to you?'

'Nothing, didn't I just say? Are youse thick or deaf or what? Now shut the fuck up, I'm gonna take forty winks until he comes. No point in worrying about what's up, 'tis soon enough we'll know, I reckon.'

He closed his eyes and Niall bit his lip. Surly bastard, he thought, never quite knew what made him tick. He was right about one thing, though– they'd just have to wait. Shouldn't be long now, surely.

Almost two hours passed. Then in the silence, they could hear the soft splash coming up river. As they listened, the splash, splash came nearer. By the time the small boat glided to a stop, they were both at the riverbank, eyes straining - the beam of Niall's torch bobbing crazily up and down on the surface of the water.

'For fuck's sake, quench the light!' The voice was harsh and furious. The moonlight was bright enough now for Niall to see the face of the man clambering onto the bank in front of him. It was a handsome face, long and narrow, with strong black eyebrows. Niall only knew him by his nick name- Valentino. He knew, though, that the handsome face was deceiving. Valentino was a ruthless bastard, had to be, to stay on top of the trade for this long. It was muttered that he'd sell his mother if the profit margin was good enough – sell her with a smile too. No one crossed Valentino. Some men had found out this to their peril – the last thing they ever found out. Niall shivered, he felt his whole body tremble. How could he ever have gotten into this?

Valentino turned back and spoke down to someone in the boat. 'Miguel,' he snapped, 'bring him out.' There were grunts and scuffles and then a dark figure appeared out of the boat, dragging something bulky behind him before flinging it down onto the path.

'What the – 'Niall looked at Miguel, then at the still figure of the man curled up on the ground and recoiled as if he'd been shot. He stepped backwards, almost losing his balance. He could feel the bile rising in his throat and, turning around, bent over and vomited on the grass. Suddenly, he felt a hard hand at his back, catching him by the collar and pulling him roughly to his feet. He looked away from the prone figure, but Miguel was behind him now, hand twisting Niall's face so that he couldn't but look at the badly broken figure, unconscious, bloodied, on the ground in front of him.

Tom, oh sweet Jesus, Tom, he thought and he swayed again.

He turned towards Valentine. He opened his mouth, but it was so dry he couldn't speak. He tried again.

'Why?' His voice was hoarse, 'why... wha, what'd he do?'

Valentine ignored the question and began speaking softly, intimately.

'Of course, you and he are friends.' Though the voice was quiet, Niall swayed again, would have fallen, except for Miguel's hand gripping him. Christ Almighty, what was going on? What had Tom done?

'Did you really think I wouldn't find out?' the voice was still soft, almost fatherly. 'One packet! Did you really think I wouldn't miss it.'

The tone continued, soft, regretful.

Niall suddenly found his voice. 'Packet, what packet? What the fuck you talking about?'

Valentino came up close, pushing his face into Niall's, stopping Niall's words

'You little shit, you stupid little shits.''. The voice was a snarl now.

The voice paused, softened again. 'Do you know what I hate above all else, hmm?'

Niall tried to speak again, thoughts racing, his mouth opened, he gabbled, couldn't stop, couldn't even understand what he was saying himself. Then he screamed as Valentino, grabbed his hair, lifting him clean off the ground.

The voice was soft now in his ear 'Stupidity. Stupid, greedy little fuckers, like you and little Tombo there.'

Valentino suddenly stilled. 'Ah Christ, the smell, the fucking smell ....'

Niall whimpered and tried to turn away to avoid the blows. There was a crunch and the blood gushed from his nose, his lip and then a high scream as the kick landed between his legs...

By the time he found himself on the ground beside Tom, Niall was only half conscious, his body a throbbing, screaming mass of pain. Above him, Valentino stepped back, breathing hard, face scrunched in revulsion and nodded to Stephen

'Don't take too long. No traces, mind'.

Stephen walked towards the two prostrate men. Behind him, Valentino was already disappearing into the boat behind Miguel.

In exactly forty minutes, by the time the bells of St. Michael's chimed 4am, Stephen was walking back through the trees. His heart was racing and though his whole body was drenched with sweat, still he was cold, icy cold. He stopped for a moment, leaning against a tree trunk to take a deep breath to steady himself. He was afraid his legs wouldn't hold him upright. He laughed shakily, no amusement in it. Jesus, he'd been lucky this time, very lucky. Behind him was an empty clearing and the river, mysterious, secretive, flowing quickly along towards the sea.

# Epiphany

When I arrived at *Bluebell Wood* for my daily walk yesterday, I was met by a very strange situation. A woman I know well, a very respectable and sensible lady, was pacing up and down beside her car, and seemed to be in the middle of some kind of emotional crisis.

When I drew up, she turned towards me with such enthusiasm that I was quite taken aback – until she saw who I was.

'Jesus,' says she. Throwing her arms up in despair and resuming her frantic walking. 'I'm looking for a man. Where in God's name are all the men of the town? I thought the place would only be crawling with them at this hour of the morning.'

'What man?' says I, still not quite getting what she was on about.

'Any man at all,' says she, nearly tearing her hair out. 'I'm in no position to be fussy.'

Then, it struck me, like a hammer blow, I actually staggered with the shock of it. The unfortunate woman was in the middle of some desperate and overwhelming attack of sexual frustration. Jeez, the hairs stood on the back of my neck at such wantonness. I mean, I'm no prude but her behaviour… I mean. To be honest, I didn't know what to do with myself. Even more blatant was the fact that this well brought- up lady had the back doors of her Fiesta wide open. There was obviously going to be very little time spent on the 'getting to know you business.' Still, maybe at this stage in life, it was permissible to cut through the preliminaries and get down to brass tacks immediately.

I was overcome by a wave of sadness. Mother of God, I thought, is this what's in store for us all when we get a bit older – skulking in the wood, at the crack of dawn, waiting to proposition, willy nilly, any stray man that happens to appear among the evergreens?

Before I could get my thoughts together, there was the sound of a vehicle approaching and my woman only turns around with the most pitiful expression of hope on her face. It was embarrassing to see. I didn't even have to look towards the new arrival to see if it was a man, because I could see from the expression of bliss on her face that her prayers had been answered. Oh yes, to my acute discomfort, it was most definitely a male who had just pulled in. Forgetting all about me, she gave a whoop of joy and made a beeline for the man emerging from the driver's seat.

Trust me, I didn't really want to witness the poor creature making a show of herself but I wasn't fast enough in covering my ears nor were my legs fast enough to get me out of there so... And then, it was too late and she'd opened her mouth to speak.

'Thank God,' says she, putting out her hands to your man, 'There's a cat trapped somewhere in my car and I've been waiting here for ages for a man who knows how to open the bonnet of a Fiesta, so I can get him out before he gets killed, or smothered or something. Shure Mary and myself are both useless. He's after coming all the way from town inside somewhere in the car. I think he must be inside the engine 'cos he's not in the front or back seats nor the boot, I've the inside searched and I've opened all the doors to give him a chance to escape but...'

What? What did the woman just say? Did she just mention a cat, like, an actual cat?

I looked at her then and the car and the man. A cat, a fecking cat! Trapped inside in her car and....

I began to get dizzy and staggered. I made it to the nearest tree and leaned up against the trunk of it.

Jesus, I must be losing my marbles altogether. I mean, imagine me thinking what I was actually thinking about an eminently respectable woman like...

My God, I've never been the same since the menopause. Maybe, I really should go on HRT, maybe... Women have been locked up for less in this country. Imagine, if Id mentioned it in a secret to any of my friends? I burst out in a renewed sweat at the thought of the consequences.

PS: The little fecker of a cat was last seen tearing up the main Street like a rocket, trying to escape his experiences in the wood – and my good kind friend, with the Fiesta. Not an ounce of appreciation for all the trouble he was after causing. Probably traumatised so approach with caution

Ah jeez, not the bleddy cat, I mean the respectable woman in the Fiesta! Devil a' fear of the bleddy cat!

# Rubber Man

The evening sunshine sparkled on the small fields stretching down the valley towards the village. Here and there, black and white cows corralled behind hedges and stone walls nibbled lazily at the grass, swishing their tails intermittently to ward off the flies.

Crossing the farmyard, Paddy Kelly didn't feel the heat nor did he see the fields or the cows below him. He was almost seventy now and a lifetime spent in Ballinacarriga, a small townland two miles from the village, had robbed him of the ability to see any beauty in either the hills or rocky fields around him.

A small thickset man with a worn tweed cap, he walked slowly, carefully. Face furrowed, eyes screwed up in concentration, scrutinising the yard as if it were peppered with mines. At last, reaching the farmhouse door, he lifted the latch and stepped into the small dark kitchen, momentarily blinded, until his eyes adjusted to the darkness after the bright sunshine outside. He bent down and eased off each boot with a low grunt placing them neatly side by side behind the kitchen door. He made his way across the floor, easing himself down with a groan into the old armchair by the window, facing down the valley.

Paddy couldn't remember now when the darkness had started inside his head, when he stopped looking out at the fields and the river. When he had last felt joy at anything or laughed from deep down his belly. Long before his mother and father had died, that was certain.

Maybe it had started when Maggie left. When they met first, he hadn't known what to make of her. She'd laughed a lot, something he wasn't used to, there wasn't much laughing at home in Ballinacarriga. Though she'd lived in the village all her life, he'd never really noticed her until the night of the barn dance when he'd twirled her round the floor for sheer devilment, until laughingly she'd begged him to stop. Sweating, he'd led her off the floor and through the swaying laughing crowd, quietly glad that his mad twirling had made her dizzy enough to need to sit down.

After the dance they'd started walking out together. With her, he'd felt a lightness that he'd never felt in the old corrugated farmhouse with his strong-willed mother and silent father who moved like a shadow around the farm.

When his mother found out that he, a farmer's son, was throwing himself away, as she'd put it, on the daughter of Donie Galvin, a labouring man, with the arse out through his trousers like all his family before him, she'd nearly thrown off her clothes with fury. She'd ranted and raved while his father stood there silent. Over her dead body she swore would a Galvin from a cottage come into the place. There was no reasoning with her and faced with her fury and threats, Paddy backed down. In truth, he hadn't tried very hard to stand up to her. He was his father's son alright, he'd thought bitterly in the long years since, no backbone.

The morning Maggie left for Chicago, something died in him. He often thought as he brought the cows in for milking or led them out after milking that all the sunshine in his life had gone with her. He began to hate his mother and father and was glad when, first his father and then his mother, were taken on their final journey down the long boreen from the house. It was then, as he tried to curb the hysterical laughter rising like a spring tide inside him, that he knew there must be something wrong with him. When the neighbours pressed their rough hands on his, telling him they were sorry for his trouble, he had to turn away to hide the triumph and relief in his eyes.

Paddy despised himself. He knew he was pathetic, no backbone to stand up for what he wanted. He'd cravenly let Maggie go – folded like a pack of cards before his mother's threats. A spineless apology for a man – like his father, rubber instead of steel in his backbone. When he heard she'd married, the light faded even more and he went about his farm duties doggedly, eyes down and silent.

It was around then that the voice in his head started.

*'Spineless Paddy, Rubber Man'*

The voice went on and on and after a while, he grew afraid of it. He'd be down at the village after Sunday Mass making small talk with the neighbours and suddenly, he'd hear it, low and mocking *'Rubber Man, Rubber Man'*. He'd come out in a sweat then and look with terror at the men he was talking to, wondering if they heard it too. Sweating, he'd mumble something and turn away in mid-conversation. One Sunday, as the sun shimmered and danced through the stained glass window behind the altar, he noticed Fr. O Mahony, smirking at him as he held up the chalice. *"Behold the blood of the Rubber Man, behold…'*

After that, he went to Mass no more.

He became obsessed with the voice. Even when it was silent, he waited for it and fretted when it didn't come. He avoided people, all his thoughts turned into his head, listening for the voice. In bed, he could only sleep for a few hours, tossing and turning and then he'd wake up, sweating, heart pounding, stomach churning. There was a manic energy inside his body that wouldn't let him rest. Sometimes, he half ran, half stumbled like a crazed man up and down the long narrow kitchen, screaming to get that terrifyingly restless energy out. It worked for a while but then built again, slowly at first and then faster and faster. And he stumbled faster, screaming into the empty air until his breath caught. Still the voice whispered, *'Rubber Man, Rubber Man, Rubber Man,'* When he fell to his knees, gasping and shaking and put trembling hands to his ears, he could still hear it *'Rubber Man, Rubber Man'*.

Sometimes he gulped down large mouthfuls of whiskey but no matter how much he drank, the voice was always there, only the words changing, 'Useless bollocks, useless bollocks, useless'. He'd tried shouting out nursery rhymes as he stumbled up and down the kitchen

Ring a ring a Rosie,

*Rubber Man, Rubber Man*

A pocket full of posies,

*Rubber Man, Rubber Man*

No, No, No! He tried to close his ears and say the words louder to drown out the chanting voice

ATISHOO, ATISHOO AND ALL FALL DOWN

*Rubber Man, Rubber Man RUBBER Maaannnnn*

In despair, he clutched his head and threw himself on the ground, tears and snot mingling. He prayed to God and all the saints, staring desperately at the Sacred Heart hanging on the wall but God didn't answer and the Scared Heart above the fireplace, smiled indifferently over his head.

But all that was a long time ago. Now Paddy mocked himself for ever fighting it, for being frightened. One morning he woke up and he was afraid no more. The voice was right; he would listen to it. Hadn't he bent like a blade of summer grass before the strength of his mother's will? He was nothing and then he knew his mother wasn't wrong at all. Shure, wasn't he the one that didn't stand up for what he wanted? 'Sorry, mammy,' he said humbly to the empty kitchen and the stern Sacred Heart on the wall above the fire.

He laughed, a high shrill sound. Afraid of his shadow, just like the voice in his head said. A Rubber Man, hiding away from the world, milking his cows and saving his hay and milking his cows and saving his hay, year in year out. What good had he ever done? What good was he doing now?

Fuck all, that's what. He listened as he said the words and giggled. His mother wouldn't like it but he didn't have to think of her anymore. He said the words again. Fuck all. He savoured the sound, yes, he liked it. Fuck all, fuck all. His voice growing louder, Jack, the black and white sheepdog, raised his head from the corner of the fire and seeing that it was only Paddy, put his face down in his paws again and closed his eyes. Paddy didn't notice. There was a look of rapture on his face as he repeated the words softer and faster – fuck all, rubber man, fuck all, bollocks.

He looked forward to hearing the voice now. It soothed him. They had long conversations together which broke the monotony of his day. He didn't want the company of the few neighbours who called sometimes of an evening, sitting by the fire and speaking in their slow voices. Their visits irritated him so he answered in monosyllables, when he could be bothered to say anything at all, until they rose, shaking their heads and went away home again over the fields.

Soon, when he saw Jamsie Connors or Timeen Leary coming across the meadow, he hid in one of the outhouses until they'd gone away again. Sometimes too, he sat in the kitchen, smiling and murmuring *'Rubber Man, Rubber Man'* as the door rattled and a voice called 'Paddy, are you there, man?' And Paddy rocked himself gently back and forth until the knocking stopped and there was only himself and the voice and the silence once more enveloping the old farmhouse like a comfortable old blanket.

As time passed a great heaviness settled on Paddy. The voice was tired too and he didn't hear it as often anymore. Daily he struggled, laboriously putting one foot in front of the other. The milking of his cows became too much bother and he sold them off one by one to neighbouring farmers. He washed less, soon stopping altogether, apart from a lick of the cloth over his face before he went to the village shop early in the morning when few people were about.

He spent more and more time inside the old farmhouse, sitting there for hours in the old chair, staring with dull eyes down the valley. Sometimes when his eyes focused, he could see the houses of the Connors, the Kellehers and the Learys, and Timeen Leary himself out there in the fields, talking, milking, saving the hay – busy, busy like so many insects scurrying hither and thither. He saw them all from a great distance, no longer part of their busy world. He realised without surprise that he hadn't been part of that world for a very long time.

His head always felt thick and heavy now. He smiled vaguely, listlessly. The *Rubber Man.* Wasn't it strange, Paddy thought, that a *Rubber Man* could be tired, like ordinary men?

Ring a ring a Rosie – *Rubber Man,*

A pocket full of posies – *for the Rubber Man*

Atishoo, atishoo,

All fall down – *Rubber Man, Rubber Man.*

The evening sunshine sparkled on the small fields stretching down the valley, glinting on the roofs of the houses in Curramore village. Raising himself from the chair, Paddy moved across towards the kitchen door, holding the coiled rope in his right hand.

The faint cries of Timeen Leary calling his cows drifted up the hillside. Inside the farmhouse, all was still. Darting ribbons of light danced around the gently swaying shadow suspended from the partially opened door. From high on the wall, where He had hung for decades past, the Sacred Heart smiled his enigmatic, merciless smile.

# Chrissie

Whenever I close my eyes. It's her hair I see first. A scarf of trapped sunlight. Then, her smile. And the way she looks at me...

It's autumn now. The lane is rutted, overgrown, jagged ribbon of grass zig- zagging through the centre. A swarm of crows reel from the trees, cackling loudly at the unexpected intrusion into their solitude.

My eyes rake the ground. Part of me expects to see traces of caravan wheels on the grass verge. But of course, there is nothing. I stand still, listening, and across the decades and into the silence comes the voice, distant, rising and falling...

'Do you live in the cottage beyond, the one by the river? '

The girl is not much older than me and carries a basket. And she is beautiful. So beautiful. A princess from the fairy tales my mother read to me as a child. Feet bare on the dusty lane, tanned legs stretching forever. She is nothing like the village girls I go around with.

Holding her head slightly to one side, she examines me, an open, unhurried look.

I say nothing. I cannot. I'm conscious that my mouth is slightly open and I snap it shut. I stare, drinking in the vision before me. I've slipped into another world, a secret place, just myself and the girl with the basket.

I cannot speak. A tremor runs through my body and my breathing quickens. My mouth is dry. My body jerks, stunned by what I find myself thinking - because I want to touch her. I want to run my fingers through the glorious hair, to caress her face. I can hardly breathe, terrified by these strange feelings.

What is happening to me?

I'm about to turn, to escape, when she speaks again.

'My name is Chrissie.'

A pause. I swallow.

'I'm Molly,' I say, finding my voice.

I'm bolder now, excited, reckless even.

I no longer want to run away.

She smiles. We smile at each other...

My hands clench. Her voice through the somersault of years.

'My name is Chrissie,'

The touch of her hands, her mouth, soft on my skin.

It's autumn now. I see her still, her smile, the sunlight in her hair.

And the way she looked at me.

# Nothing is, But What is Not

Wednesday, November 7th, 1940

The ten Victorian cottages in London's East End had been completely flattened. Flames still shot upwards intermittently as rescue workers fanned out cautiously over the mountains of rubble that was now all that remained of St. George's Terrace.

Stan Oldfield, sweat trickling down his blackened face, had joined the auxiliary fire service at the outbreak of war the year before. Now he moved carefully. If, by some miracle, there was anyone alive underneath the tons of debris, the least movement might bring everything tumbling down on top of them. Hard to believe that only a few hours before, over sixty people, had lived and laughed here.

Suddenly there was a shout.

'Over 'ere, Stan.'

A great cloud of dust obscured his vision for a moment and when it cleared, he could see the men carrying a body. His lips tightened. Since the Luftwaffe began their murderous blitz on London in early September, Stan reckoned he'd seen every horror there was to see but it didn't matter how many times he saw scenes like this, he could never get immune to it. An old man – face covered with a smattering of white dust, was the first. The next hours passed in a blur, body after body, thirty- four in all. Eight of them children, Stan tried not to think but it was hard not to scream and curse at the God that allowed this to happen to innocent people.

'Stan, 'ey Stan.' The voice was urgent.

'Someone's down there,' Reg pointed with a shaking finger. 'I can 'ear 'im. Listen.'

They huddled round a narrow black opening in the rubble.

Nothing.

Stan was just about to turn away when he stiffened.

Pushing his head through, he called 'Holla, holla, can you 'ear me?'

He heard it again, a thin cry. When he turned back, the men were huddled anxiously behind him.

In minutes, Stan, rope around his waist and flash-lamp in hand was being lowered, the light of the lamp flickering eerily in the inky blackness. An eternity passed before the men felt the strain on the rope again. They waited in silence as Stan emerged, gasping, breathless, out of the darkness.

'Two young 'uns and their mother,' His voice was hoarse, uneven. 'Lads seem alright, dunno about the mother. Trapped under timber, don't know if she can be got out. Couldn't get near enough.'

Sensing there was something more, no one spoke. 'Timber will go any minnit. …' He stopped. 'We need to get in there and quick, attach a rope to pull 'em up,' he paused again, 'thing is, where they're trapped, space's too narrow for me to squeeze through any further.'

He looked at the tense dust - streaked faces before him.

'Even if one of us manages to get through, I'm not sure they'll make it back out, whole place is about to collapse.'

In the middle of the group of men, Harry Mckenna smiled. At last, at long last, a chance to exorcise the ghosts that haunted his every moment for over twenty years. It was more than he deserved, he knew. His face twisted, remembering another time and place. He should have stood his ground then, like a man, taken what was coming to him – like Hanley, whatever else he had been, he was no coward anyway. No, He should never have run. When he spoke now, his voice was firm.

'I'll go, I'm thin enough at any rate.'

Stan turned towards the soft voice with the hint of humour and saw a smallish man, with a worn face and tired eyes. A quiet man, Irish, kept himself to himself. Stan had never seen Harry show fear in all the time they'd known him. A good man in an emergency, strong, dependable.

No one wasted time arguing. They'd been too long at this job to doubt Stan's word. Within minutes, rope around his waist, Harry was being hoisted down into the blackness. The men, grim and silent, fed the rope out. At first, they could hear Harry as he went down but after a while, there was nothing to be heard at all.

It was half an hour, one of the longest half hours the men had lived through, when they felt the stir on the rope.

'Easy, lads, easy, now.'

The boy suddenly appeared, first his head, then his shoulders. He was very young, ten at most, face covered in scratches and underneath his torn short trousers, his knees were bloody and covered in dirt.

'Awright, son, yer safe now,' Reg's voice was gentle.

The boy grinned shakily through his dust-streaked face before being taken away. The men took up their positions and endured another agonising wait before they felt the tug again. In a few minutes, another boy appeared. Clothes ripped and torn, dusty face screwed up with anxiety.

When he saw them, he began to speak, urgently, words tumbling over each other.

'Me mam, mister, me mam, she can't move, she's stuck,' His voice became shrill 'She'll die, mister, she's gonna die,' His voice broke on a sob.

'Other bloke, 'e made me go. 'e said 'e'd get 'er out.'

His voice was hoarse, agitated.

Stan patted his shoulder. 'Harry'll get 'er out, lad, never you fear.'

With the boy safely away, the men settled anxiously at the edge of the opening, trying to imagine what was happening below. The minutes passed – slowly, slowly. Then, almost out of hope, they felt the rope jerk, weakly at first and then more strongly and began to haul again…


The creaking and shifting of the timbers was much louder now. Harry knew he had to hurry. The trapped woman was very near to losing control, Harry could hear it in her voice, the hysteria just there, below the surface. God knows, he thought, who could blame her? But he had to keep her calm, her life depended on it.

'What's your name, Missus?' he called now.

There was a pause and then 'Gladys. Gladys Price'

Another pause. 'Wot's yours then?'

There was silence for a moment. 'Harry…'

He paused and began again, voice stronger,' My name is Tom, Tom O Brien,'

He listened to the sound and nodded in satisfaction. No more running.

"Can't move, the timbers, they.... they're on top of me, They're gonna smother me...'

Her voice rose shrilly.

'I'll get you out'. His voice was calm, authoritative. 'I promise you, Gladys. Listen to me now, lass. I'm gonna lift one of these timbers pinning you down. Soon's it starts moving, you gotta start crawling, but slow and careful, mind, else you'll bring the whole lot down. Can you do that, Gladys, can you crawl out while I hold up the beam?'

There was a silence. Then the voice, calmer

'You hold that beam, Mister, and I'll get out, never you fear'

'Remember now, lass, slow and careful. Soon's you're out, you'll see from the light of my lamp the rope on the ground beside me, Wind that round your waist and then, give it a jerk and they'll begin to pull you up. You got that, Gladys?'

'Yis, yis,' the woman's voice was eager now, determined.

Taking a deep breath, he felt his muscles strain as his hands tightened on the beam. Dear God in heaven, it was heavy. For a moment, just a flicker of a moment, he felt fear, fear that he'd fail the woman depending on him- like he'd failed before and then, just as suddenly, the fear vanished.

No, this time, Tom O Brien would not fail.

*County Limerick, Southern Ireland. April 1920.*

It was a glorious Sunday afternoon. Spirits were high in the long- deserted farmhouse deep in the countryside, a few miles from the small village of Curramore. Ten IRA volunteers had just finished dinner and were packing up to return to their units. Their training officers had left earlier that morning well pleased with the progress of the young men over the previous month.

The War of Independence had been going on over a year now. The young volunteers felt strong and confident after the month long training camp. That Sunday afternoon, they were rearing to go back to their battalions and do their bit. The sooner they did, the sooner, they'd be free from British rule. They could shoot and load and kill. They could strip down a rifle in minutes. They could hit any target, whether moving or stationary with a very high level of accuracy and precision. Twelve hours a day, every day, they had practised. In the beginning, all they could do was grab a bite of supper and roll into makeshift beds in the large empty farmhouse. They saw nobody except their camp leaders, tough men who trained them to kill the enemy and to try and stay alive themselves. Once only had they seen anyone, in the distance, a lone man fishing peacefully on the banks of the Blackwater.

'Jasus, the woman who marries you will have her work cut out for her,' laughed Sean Barry, as a red haired lad with an open freckled face dropped a plate on the stone floor where it smashed into smithereens.

'Well, aren't you the great catch yourself now?'' scoffed Ned Brown, stooping to pick up the pieces. 'Anyway,' he winked 'I've other talents, boy,'

Sean laughed.

'Oh, Jasus, I nearly forgot,' Ned continued,' I owe Tom a shilling after that auld card game last night. If I don't give it to him, shure, I'll never hear the end of it. He'll be telling everyone that Cork men are as tight as a duck's arse'

He looked around.

'Where is he anyway? I haven't seen him for a while.'

'Sentry duty, he went down the lane there a while back to relieve Willie.'

'Might as well take a dander down so while we're waiting for the order to go.'

Ned turned as he spoke, 'Shure, I'm packed and all ready to go anyway.'

'We'll all be off shortly,' Sean gave a glance round, 'nearly done here.'

They had strict orders to leave the old farmhouse as they'd found it, with no sign of habitation just in case the Tans found the place.

The lane was about half a mile long. A hare couldn't get past without being seen so there wouldn't be much chance for a lorry load of Tans to slip unnoticed up from the village and surprise them. Anyone looking down the valley had a clear view of the village below and the surrounding countryside for miles around. Ned whistled as he walked. He had gone less than a quarter of a mile when he stopped abruptly.

'Jesus Christ Almighty,' His face whitened.

Turning quickly, he raced back the way he had come, screaming a warning to the lads, knowing even as he did that he was too late, far too late. From the heavy drone lumbering behind him, he knew the Crossley Tenders were almost at the farmhouse gap already. He burst through the front door, the others, hearing nothing, whirled startled.

'Tans, Tans,' he gasped' get out, quick, for fuck's sake.'

'What the…?'

'But how the hell…?

Then the heavy trundling of lorries broke the silence of the farmyard and grabbing rifles, some volunteers made for the windows, smashing glass. Others were still scrambling for their guns, slow to grasp the reality of the Tans' presence so fast had things happened. One moment laughing and joking, packing bags and talking about future meetings and then …

'We have you surrounded,' the English voice was cold, precise.' You have one minute to surrender, then we open fire.'

'Surrender, bollocks.' shouted Barry from the window. The Volunteers began firing and in a moment, the peace of the afternoon was punctured by gunfire. The Tans were well prepared. Before the three Crossley Tenders had entered the farmyard, over two dozen men had jumped off and spread out around the farmhouse. The volunteers were caught, like rats in a trap, completely surrounded. A young lad, no more than seventeen, lay white faced and whimpering, eyes bulging with terror on the floor where he had fallen, blood spurting from his stomach.

Ned Brown was the most senior volunteer there. He looked at the young lad as the blood pumped onto the floor.

'Mick,' he jumped down beside him, 'you'll be alright, boy.'

Even as he caught the bloodied hand in a tight grip, the body on the ground jerked feebly and was still. Over at one of the windows, Pat, a stocky lad from Curramore village, was firing, reloading and firing, oblivious of the blood trickling from his shoulder. From other rooms around the house, it was the same story. Ned looked around. Jesus Christ!

He dropped to his knees.

'Almost out of ammo, Ned'' Pat continued firing as he spoke through gritted teeth. Ned nodded and crawled frantically into the other rooms. It was the same everywhere. Ammunition almost gone. Two choices, Ned gasped. Either make a run for it or surrender. No fucking choice! They were surrounded, heavily outnumbered and would be mown down like rats in a hay-barn. No point in giving the bastards the satisfaction of shooting 'em in the back.

Some of the lads were crying with rage and helplessness as Ned gave the order to stop firing. When the Tans realised that firing from inside the farmhouse had ceased, they stopped shooting as well but stayed well out of sight. The silence was broken by Ned.

'We're coming out,' he yelled' don't shoot.'

'Right.' It was the same English voice as before.' Leave your guns inside the house. On the count of three, come out with your hands up. Any tricks and we'll shoot.'

Inside the farmhouse, no one spoke. One by one, the volunteers lined up, their guns a neat pile on the floor behind them. Before opening the door, they shook hands and slapped each other on the back. One of the lads walked over to where Mick lay and kneeling, touched the black curls gently, briefly.

Then Ned faced them. A nerve twitched in his cheek, but his voice was steady enough.

'We'll fight again. Now, shoulders straight. Walk tall, volunteers.'

The sunlight blinded them as they emerged from the farmhouse. They blinked as shadows uncoiled from behind the lorries. There were at least twenty Tans. Out of the corner of his eye, Ned saw more figures spread out to the side of the house.

'Right, stand in a straight line.' The officer, a stocky man, held a pistol in his left hand. The volunteers lined up next to each other. Sean was next to Ned.

'Where the hell is Tom?' he muttered.

Now that the fighting was over and they had a chance to think, Ned wondered about that too. At the sentry post, there was a clear view of anything moving in the direction of the old farmhouse. Anyone watching down the valley would have seen the Tans once they came into the village. Plenty of time to give warning and get out. So what the fuck had happened and where was Tom?

The officer moved back towards the lorries before stopping.

'Ready, aim, '

'What the...'

'Fire!'

Some of the volunteers didn't have time to realise what was happening before the bullets struck. Then there was only the noise of the lorries turning in the old farmyard before lumbering slowly out the gap and down the narrow winding road towards Curramore. Behind them, in the lazy heat of the Sunday afternoon, there was only silence…


Tom O Brien hated sentry duty. Nothing to do except look out for enemies that didn't even know they were there. He was thirsty, the river, where they had got their water for the last month, straggling away two fields below him in the valley, beckoned. Shure, no one knew about the training camp. Hadn't they been there for a month - if the Tans knew, they wouldn't have waited weeks. The bastards would have attacked long before now. They'd all be gone their separate ways in an hour, back to their units to kill as many of the murdering bastards as they could. Anyway, he'd fill his water bottle, have a cool drink and still be back inside twenty minutes. Who'd be any the wiser? He was jumping down from the ditch before he'd finished the thought.

There was no trace of the lone fisherman on the river-bank that Sunday afternoon. Instead, following a warning from the British, former private John Hanley, ex Munster Fusiliers stayed home in his small cottage. He'd fought in the trenches, had been almost killed at the Somme. He'd returned home with a useless hand and a crippled mind. Most nights, he woke screaming and sweating. The horrors of France so real that he'd stumble from bed and sit shivering in the chair staring unseeing into the darkness until daybreak. Hanley had no time for these farm-boy killers, hiding behind ditches to do their dirty work. Where were they when he was fighting in the slaughterhouse of France? At home in fucking safety, that's where…

Tom was lying full stretch on the river-bank when he heard the first barrage of gunfire from the direction of the old farmhouse. He stilled, water spilling out of cupped palms …

The rope was heavy and in a few minutes, the men's faces glistened with perspiration and then suddenly, she was there, the woman, appearing out of the shadows, in front of them. Her face grimacing in pain as they helped her gently through the opening.

'Collapsed,' she explained feebly, peering at the faces above her. 'Beam, that man, Tom, 'e 'eld the beam,' she gasped for breath, 'while I crawled out and then, then…'

She paused and began to cry weakly.

''e saved my life, that man, he saved my life.'

## The Country Boy

It was cold, bitterly cold. Inside the brightly lit stores seasonal music blared above the clattering of cash registers as the crowds jostled each other in the mad scramble for last minute bargains.

Outside the heaving stores, the street lights winked and shone through the gloom of the December afternoon. The hum of voices, the gaily decorated windows and the giant Christmas tree at the top of Pearse Street all created a feeling of good will, despite the chill of the wintry evening.

At the corner of the street, the old man hunched deeper into his threadbare coat in an attempt to shut out the worst of the bitter wind blowing diagonally across the bridge. People hurried past, all on their way somewhere. Now and then, someone paused, fumbled briefly in handbags and pockets, threw a coin or two into the old cardboard box, before continuing on their way again. Crossing the bridge, a young man in a long blue scarf, threw back his head laughing loudly at something his friend said. The old man's eyes were dreamy as he watched the young men until they disappeared from view. Had there ever really been a time, he wondered, when he had been that young and carefree?

*'Granda, what about that one? Look at the lovely juicy berries on it!'*

*Eagerly, the young boy clambered up the ditch while behind him, the old man, his grandfather, advised caution. 'Aisy, Joe, aisy, take your time now, lad,'*

*Carefully, the boy, reached out and began breaking off sprigs from the holly tree, rich with blood red berries. His grandfather watched, smiling at the lad's enthusiasm – the boy was slow at the* book learning, but shure, what harm, he thought, as long as he has the bit of land, he'll never starve.

'When you were young, did you gather holly like this, Granda?' Joe knew the answer well but he never tired of hearing those tales of long ago.

'Ah, it's well I remember my brother Tim and myself and a couple of the village lads, traipsing through snow and sludge and rain and wind to this very wood and then when we could carry no more, we'd stagger home as proud as punch, arms loaded with holly.' Granda's voice grew soft with memory. On they walked companionably, the old man and the young boy, pushing the old handcart laden with holly between them, breaths small clouds in the nippy air around them.

Christmas Eve in the old farmhouse with the corrugated roof was glorious – the big kitchen filled with warmth and his mother bustling about saying she'd 'never have it all done on time' But shure, it always was and long before darkness fell, the big goose would lay plucked and bare on the pine table, the smell of cooking would wrap itself around the kitchen and the big barmbrack, only ever baked once a year, at Christmas, would be stacked safely out of harm's way beside the old orange vases on the dresser. There'd be sprigs of holly hanging from the Sacred Heart and the Blessed Mother and all the other holy pictures dotted around the walls so that the whole kitchen was completely transformed from what it looked like every other day of the year.

On Christmas Eve, neighbours and relations called to the house on their way to Midnight Mass in the village and soon, the kitchen echoed with laughter and stories of long ago. Great Aunt Kate, toothless and wrinkled sat by the bellows, wrapped, as always, in her heavy black shawl. Around the fire, the grown-ups talked of times past and the old friends who'd passed on since the previous Christmas. The flames from the turf fire threw leaping shadows on the walls and the candle in the hollowed out turnip in the window *flickered and glowed and threw a welcoming light to all who passed along the darkness of the quiet road outside.*

*And in the morning, the stockings hanging at the foot of the bed bulged. One Christmas, he'd got a coloured drum and he'd marched proudly around for weeks with it, never leaving it out of his sight in case it vanished.*

*The passing of years brought with them the inevitable changes. Granda had long passed away when Tom, always the brighter and his father's favourite, left for America. 'There's nothing for me here, Dada,' he'd repeated over and over and he stood firm despite his mother's tears and his father's pleading.*

*Nothing was the same after Tom left but the change in his father was shocking. He grew bitter and short-tempered and impossible to please. There were frequent quarrels. When Joe was nervous, he made mistakes and the more his father shouted and ranted at him, the more mistakes he made. He could do nothing right. And then that last row – Joe couldn't even remember what it was about now. He could recall the harsh words and the vicious blows though and the icy contempt in his father's voice 'Get outa here, you useless amadán you,' he'd shouted' and don't ever darken the door again.'*

So he went, his mother's cries ringing in his ears and was too proud to return when his father's temper would have had a chance to cool down.

To a country lad, the city was huge – huge and unfriendly. Among all the hundreds of people, not a single kindly face. In the beginning, he only went to the pub for company and warmth, anything was better than his cold empty room. After a while, he discovered that a couple of drinks softened the bare room and warmed him inside. It even dulled his loneliness – for a while anyway.

It wasn't long before jobs became scarce – he was too unreliable. Soon, he was drinking more and more to shut out those memories he couldn't cope with when he was sober.

Once he nearly went home. For three whole days he'd stayed clear of the bottle and then, glancing at a store window he'd seen what others saw – a waster, and he heard his father's voice ringing in his ears as clearly as if he stood beside him and he knew he couldn't go back, not yet. And then, it was too late, his mother died and he cursed himself for every kind of fool…

The old man shivered. God, it was cold. Night had fallen now and the crowds had all but disappeared. Slowly he got to his feet and with an unsteady hand picked up the cardboard box. Rattling the box, he sighed gently and then turning, he trudged off slowly into the darkness beyond the bridge.

Faintly from across the river wafted the strains of carol singers

*Hark the Herald Angel singing*

*Glory to the New Born King*

*Peace on Earth*

*Goodwill to men…*

# Jimmy's Cross

September 1971

The moonlight lit up the small road ahead so that it could almost be day. Suddenly, less than a hundred yards away, a man came out of the shadows of the oak trees lining the road on both sides. As the figure neared, Tom's knees almost buckled and he opened his mouth to scream but no sound emerged. He tried to run but whatever way he turned he found his way blocked by that dark smirking face. Smirking, always smirking, always before him. Then the face changed and blood streamed from the nose, the eyes but the figure staggered on…

Rays of sunlight flickered through the partially opened window. It threw dancing shadows around the small statue of the Sacred Heart on the narrow shelf over the bed where Tom Doherty lay. Lollipop stick hands clutched the top of the faded blue and pink blanket. Darting eyes in a face sunken and yellow and sparsely covered in thin grey stubble.

From the kitchen, just along the narrow hallway, came the clatter of dishes and muted voices. But here in the bedroom, under the faded blanket, Tom was deaf to the sounds, eyes fixed on the narrow window, hands convulsively grasping the blanket. He shuddered and a low moan gargled deep in his throat. In a few minutes, despite himself, his eyes began to close and again the smirking face was before him. He writhed feebly and uselessly and the thin scream caught in his throat. Then, the face was before him again, bloodied, eyes closed and crusted, nose pulped, yet still that grotesque smirk on the torn lips.

'No, no,' Tom whimpered. He struggled to clamber out of the bed just as Kitty, his daughter-in-law ran in.

'It's all right, Tom,' she soothed the old man as his hand gripped hers with a strength that belied the cancer ravaging his body. There was a sheen of sweat on his thin face and spittle at the side of his mouth. He mumbled something she couldn't make out. Worn out from his struggle, the old man sagged back against the pillow, still clutching her hand and staring beyond her with terror- filled eyes.

Friday, March 24th 1922

It was nearing 11 o clock in O' Callaghan's pub just outside the small village in County Limerick. Soon be time to close, Mick Callaghan thought, as he looked at the old clock on the wall behind the bar. The few customers nursed their pints around the turf fire. They were talking quietly among themselves. There hadn't been many in that night. There was a growing helplessness and anger in the country – an ugliness, Mick thought as he washed off the few glasses and replaced them on a shelf, an ugliness that was dangerous. The treaty, ending the struggle for Irish freedom had only been signed before Christmas. Since then, up and down the country people were divided between those who supported it despite its limitations and those who saw it as a betrayal of everything they'd fought for. Everywhere, the anti and pro- treaty supporters were squaring up to each other. Less than two weeks ago, when the British had moved out of Limerick Barracks, the anti- treaty boys had nipped in smartly before the pro- treaty government forces could take the barracks over. Two weeks later the standoff was still going on between them and the government forces. The poor bastards in the Provisional Government were powerless and if the anti- treaty boys didn't pull back people didn't know where it would all end. Christ, Mick thought, it was easier when the Tans were here, at least then we were all on the same side.

In these dangerous times, people were in no mood to venture out. Look at tonight, only a few in. Willie and Seamie Connors from just below the village and young Tom Doherty and Tim Newman, a cattle dealer from up the hill. An angry man, young Tom, thought Mick looking at his sullen face. No lover of the treaty. He'd been out in the campaign and felt bitterly let down by what they'd ended up with. He was only in tonight to have a farewell drink for Willie Connors, off to Boston on Saturday. Willie was another bitterly disappointed man, he couldn't live, he said, in a country whose leaders had betrayed the republic. Mick sighed, another young fella gone. And all the lads lost in the Tan War, nine from the parish alone. Mick wasn't too happy with the treaty himself but what they had now was a damm sight more than what they had to begin with and shure, please God, like Collins said, it was only a stepping stone to full independence. Whatever people's feelings, surely to God 'twas time to call a halt to the madness of killing and mayhem.

Mick's lips tightened as he looked at Tim Newman. He'd had a skinful and no mistake. Mick hadn't realised when he came in that he'd already called to a few pubs in the village on his way home from the fair in Tullybawn. Now he could hear his voice rising. 'Another round there, Mick, before we go, shure, we'll toast the brave boys who fought for Ireland.' he called, voice slurred. One by one the lads demurred. But Tim insisted. He drew out a wallet with a flourish. Jasus, Mick saw the wad of notes. Must be money in cattle, he thought sourly, more then there is in pint pulling, that's for sure. He looked over at the boys. More than fighting for freedom too, by the looks of things. He sighed again. He pulled the pints and took them over to the small table by the fire.

'Sláinte, lads' Tim raised his glass, hand shaking slightly. He looked at young Doherty. 'To the treaty and the Free State', he mocked 'and to Collins and all our brave boys who bate the English back home.'

Tom forced himself to say nothing. Flushing, he grabbed his drink and raised his glass in Tim's direction. He wouldn't give the auld bastard the soot of riling him. Nothing in his face betrayed the thoughts going round in his head. He was sickened by the treaty. He felt Collins and the others should be shot as traitors. Had they fought and died and murdered and done things that his mind shied away from for a Free fucking State? To carve up the country and swear loyalty to the fucking English king? He bloody well hadn't, that was for sure.

The Dohertys farmed a few acres just outside the village. The land was poor and the struggle to make a living was constant. Tom was the only one left at home now. His five siblings were long gone, scattered to the four winds. Séan in Boston working on the railways. Mary and Joan in Liverpool, Paddy in Oregon and Séamus in London. They'd never come back. Why would they? What was for them here only slavery and hunger?

He should have gone himself but he was seduced by the republican dream, eejit that he was. He'd thought things would be different if he joined the Volunteers and forced the English out, that his children and their children would be free in their own country, in a republic, not a fucking Free State and the bastards still holding on to six Northern counties.

As he saw Timeen flashing his wallet with the wad of notes in it, his thoughts were bitter. Timeen and others like him hadn't been out, no, they'd stayed at home, cowering under the bedclothes while lads like himself and the others risked everything going from safe house to safe house, all the time one step ahead of the murdering Tans. What was their reward after all that? Maybe, he thought bitterly, Timeen and others like him were the sensible ones. As he listened to the drunken voice taunting him, he had an almost uncontrollable urge to put his fist through the auld sleveen's face and smash every bone in his body. He looked contemptuously at Timeen's flushed face, heard the strident, jeering voice. As he sat there brooding and sipping his pint, the voices around him faded into a low indistinct mumble. What good was money like that to someone like Timeen? He had neither chick nor child to look after. What he could do with it in his few acres beyond the village. Life was a bad joke. Look at himself risking everything, being hunted down like an animal and Timeen making money hand over fist all that time. A big cattle dealer. Shure, everyone knew he was loaded. Mind you, the devil the good he did with it. Apart from having a skinful now and again after a profitable fair day, there wasn't the spending of a tanner in him. Hungry old bastard.

Draining the last of the porter, Tom abruptly stood up. 'I'm off, lads,' There was a flurry of activity. The Connors brothers stood up too. 'Shure, it's late' Willie said 'time we all got going.'

Timeen said nothing but sat rocking backwards and forwards staring into the dying embers as the lads shouted their farewells and left. Outside the door of the pub, the cold frosty air hit them like a belt from a hurley. They shivered and shuffled their feet, not knowing what to say now that the parting was on them. Then Tom patted Willie's shoulder awkwardly with one hand.

'Mind yourself, man.'

Willie gripped him hard by the hand but said nothing, quickly turning away with a silent Séamus following behind him.

Tom watched them go, he had a lump in his throat. He'd known the lads all his life, sat beside Willie at school, joined the Volunteers together, soldiered together in the Flying Column. Suddenly, he felt the rage almost overwhelming him. He stood there for a moment longer. When he could no longer hear the sound of their boots clattering on the road, he turned himself for home.

He'd only travelled about a quarter of a mile when he stopped abruptly. He looked at the sky above him. Fucking Free State. The Limerick lads were right to stand up for themselves. Willie gone, no chance of a republic, bastards like Timeen laughing and scoffing at them. He stood immobile for a few moments and his face hardened, turning ugly. Abruptly, decisively, he leapt over the ditch, the moonlight showing the way clearly in front of him.

He moved swiftly. People living up the hill often used Taylor's field as a shortcut to and from the village. Just over five minutes later, he was climbing out over the gate near Jimmy's Cross. after first listening carefully to make sure there was no one on the road. He needn't have worried, it was like a graveyard, no one abroad at all at this hour of a frosty night. Crossing the small road, he took the little boreen leading up the hill. The little road was tree lined and very dark in places where the branches had grown across the path and met in a tunnel in the middle. He walked softly and after about four hundred yards he left the road altogether and veered off towards the lines of trees along the hedgerows. Concealing himself behind a copse of large oak, he settled down to wait. He was well used to waiting behind ditches, after all, he thought with a sudden flash of grim humour.

Tim Newman's badly beaten body was discovered by a farm labourer, shortly before noon the following day. There was great revulsion in the aftermath of the immediate discovery but it gradually died away. The village, like so many other villages, throughout the country after the War of Independence, had become almost immune to violent death and besides, within weeks of Tim Newman's murder, civil war had broken out all over the country. By the time the vicious and bloody conflict ended in May 1923, it had taken more lives than had been lost in the War of Independence. In this context, the life of one insignificant civilian, beaten to death just before the madness was unleashed, was lost among the hundreds of those killed and executed in an eleven- month orgy of rage and bitter disillusionment.

Willie Connors settled in Boston and never returned to Ireland. His brother Seamie took the anti- treaty side in the Civil War and was killed in a shoot- out with Free State soldiers on a hillside somewhere in North Cork. Tom Doherty took no part in the

Civil War and never again got involved in politics, concentrating on building up his small farm outside the village.

In the village, Tim Newman was spoken about in whispers at first and then as time moved on, not at all. The locals wondered what really happened on the night Tim was murdered. And watching Tom Doherty over the years as he expanded his few boggy fields into a sweet little farm of over sixty acres, they felt they had their answer…

Hail Mary full of grace,

The Lord is with Thee

Blessed are Thou among women…

In the weak spring sunshine, Tom Doherty's coffin, draped in the tricolour was shouldered to Robin Hill cemetery, just over a mile outside the village. The last four pall bearers hoisted the coffin, grunting quietly as they settled the weight comfortably on their shoulders. With only the soft murmuring of the rosary and the plod of hundreds of feet breaking the silence, the coffin moved out from under the shadows of the great oaks at Jimmy's Cross.

# A Night in September

Sunday, September 15$^{th}$ 1991.

*Nottingham, England.*

I am no longer young. I sit in a soft chair in the airy light-filled lounge of Altamont Lodge Nursing Home. Through the veranda window I watch the beech trees slope gently down the lawns towards the river, sunshine tripping lightly on the grass.

I am afraid, however, that today, neither the sunshine, welcome though it is, nor the beautiful beeches hold my attention for long. Since I was sixteen years old, September 15$^{th}$ has belonged to the ghosts of the past and those voices travelling across the decades clamour to be heard. Time has brought me no ease. But then, considering all that has happened, perhaps, that is as it should be.

I have not seen my home, Mount Plummer House in Southern Ireland, since I was sixteen years old. My family, the Lees, no longer farm in the village of Curramore. They have not done so since the autumn of 1920. Indeed, as the last surviving member of the family, the Lee name will die with me. Mount Plummer Estate itself is no more, having long since being broken up and divided amongst neighbouring farmers. Now, as I think of my childhood home, my fingers convulsively smooth the piece of paper on my lap.

Father was in his late fifties when I was born, Mother much younger, in her thirties. She was a Larkin whose family had farmed in the next parish of Tulla for generations. Of course, the Larkins, unlike the Lees, were not extensive landowners and it was certainly a feather in the Larkin cap when Father's eye rested on Emily, their youngest daughter. Despite the age difference, there were no objections to the match and she and my father were married in

Curramore Parish Church on August 30rd 1885. Mother was then eighteen years old and Father just over forty. She quickly bore him two sons, William and Morgan. In the summer of 1904, the year I was born, eighteen-year old William, who would succeed Father to Mount Plummer Estate in due course, was away at University while Morgan at seventeen, was being prepared for entry to the national seminary in Maynooth. I rather imagine that news of my imminent arrival caused something of a shock to both my parents and brothers that spring of 1904.

Be that as it may, in the afternoon of July 29th 1904, in the west facing bedroom of Mount Plummer House I, Josephine Ellen, was born, the last child and only daughter, of William Charles Lee, largest landowner in the parish (one didn't quite count the Protestant Lord Smithson on whose land Curramore village was built)

Servants made for a smooth running household at Mount Plummer House. Our family travelled to Mass at Curramore Church a half mile away in a spanking pony and trap where we prayed in our own pew. Most of the people around us lived in bulging little cottages along the sides of the road and the men doffed their caps as we clip clopped by in our pony and trap on Sundays. Our lives and the lives of these unfortunate people with downcast eyes and flocks of children were quite separate.

'Lees have been here for centuries' Father frequently reminded us.

The first Lee, William, arrived in Wexford with the army of the Earl of Pembroke, better known in Ireland as Strongbow, in 1170. Father was quite touchingly proud of the family name and had little time for what he termed 'nationalist nonsense.' He scoffed at the mere idea that the Irish peasant could govern himself outside of the benevolent embrace of the mighty British Empire. Poor, poor Father.

By the summer of 1920 when I was sixteen, the country was in a state of serious unrest. The Army of the Irish Republic or 'gangs of armed murderers' as Father contemptuously derided them, was attacking British Forces all over Ireland. Father was quite relieved when additional crown troops had arrived in the barracks in Tullybawn, three miles from Curramore. He was not quite so happy when some of our farmyard workers, mostly drawn from the little cottages sprinkled around the village, stopped working for us without warning.

'Gone to join the IRA murder gangs, no doubt,' he said scathingly. And then one day, Mort Neill left. Father thought a great deal of Mort who had a wonderful way with horses. Once, when Pippa, the grey pony that I'd been given for my ninth birthday, got very sick, it was Mort who somehow pulled her through. On father's insistence, Mort now accompanied Mother and I when we went riding during the glorious weather we were blessed with that year.

One morning when I went to the stable, Mort wasn't there. There was only old Con Sheehy, silent and slow. That evening at supper, I asked Father what had happened to Mort.

'Mort Neill is no better than any of the others, I'm afraid,' his voice was cold with disappointment. 'Simply disappeared without a word of explanation.'

Clenching his knife in his right hand, he added 'We will not speak of him again,'

As the summer passed, ambushes became more frequent. The IRA grew bolder and attacks were made on the military in broad daylight. In July, an ambush took place less than a mile from the village. Two soldiers were killed and three more wounded. After that, Father forbade Mother and me to go riding out of sight of the house. William, who was to take over the day to day running of the estate in the autumn, spent the summer of 1920 travelling in Italy with a friend from his army days. Father, meanwhile, was relishing those last few months in charge before William came home. He busied himself with estate business and though Mother and I worried constantly for his safety, he rode out daily after lunch to inspect the outlaying lands, sometimes not returning to the house until just before dinner.

On the 3rd of August, the trundling of army lorries down the road outside the house broke the lazy silence of the golden afternoon. From the front lawn, I counted five coming from the direction of Glean na gCapall, a beautiful lonely glen bordering Father's lands to the north. Throughout the evening and well into the night, there was constant movement of military around the village. Just before dusk, a lorry of silent soldiers, heavily armed, roared up the avenue and a tall officer, with a slight limp, got out and demanded to see Father. Shortly afterwards, the Crossley Tender belched back down the avenue again, in a smothering cloud of black smoke.

The following morning, Father was not present at breakfast when a red-eyed Hannah, our kitchen maid, told us that the soldiers had surprised and surrounded IRA men on a training camp in an old derelict farmhouse up by Killala Heights. Fourteen young lads had been surrounded and shot dead, Hannah said.

'Shure, some of the poor boys had no weapons at all and tried to give up,' her eyes welled, 'but them murdering Tans kept firing until they were all killed, may God rest 'em all'

She was sure Madam and Miss would like to know, seeing that we had been so fond of him, that Mort Neill had been one of those murdered in cold blood. Mother and I sat silent as Hannah hurried from the room, weeping. Neither of us said anything for a long time. I felt quite sick. Apart from a muttered 'Stupid young fools,' Father said remarkably little either when he arrived home later in the morning.

To our surprise, the shootings had a dreadful effect on Father. Of course, quite apart from Mort Neill, he knew some of the young local men who'd been shot and the deserted old farmhouse, where the shooting had taken place, bordered Mount Plummer lands. The day after the killings, he had quietly raged at the imprudence of the IRA in taking on the might of the Empire. After that he mentioned them no more.

But he changed - almost imperceptibly at first. He took to spending hours in his study, leaving instructions not to be disturbed. He no longer rode out over the estate and grew quiet and at times, distracted. At dinner, we often had to repeat questions while he looked at us as though we were speaking a strange language.

And then it was September. The summer had slipped away, spilling over into autumn before we had quite realised it. I remember September 15$^{th}$ 1920 quite clearly. It was a Wednesday. That week, Mother was absent from home, staying with her friends, the Laceys, in Limerick city for a few days.

Shortly after 10 o clock that Wednesday evening, I retired to bed after first kissing Father good-night. The light in the hall was dim and as I crossed towards the staircase, Hannah was opening the front door. There was a low murmur of voices. I was surprised. I wondered who could be calling so late in the evening. Father had not said he was expecting visitors. Curious, I stood in the shadows of the landing and saw a British officer, tall, dressed in leggings and trench coat, follow Hannah across the hall and into the drawing room.

The officer's face, however, I couldn't quite see because the tasselled beret he wore obscured it...

I sit and stare now across the lawn for a long time. It is only when the beating of my heart slows that I glance at the paper in my hand. It is a short article from the *Limerick Leader* newspaper, dated Friday September 17$^{th}$ 1920. The cold, matter of fact words convey little of the anguish and shock of Father's family, neither does it convey anything of the shock and anguish that I still feel over seventy years later. I hold the yellowing paper and try to still my shaking hand…

*PROMINENT COUNTY LIMERICK LANDOWNER ABDUCTED AND SHOT DEAD.*

*The body of Mr. William Lee (74), abducted from his home at Mount Plummer House near Curramore Village, Co. Limerick, late on Wednesday September 15$^{th}$, was found yesterday adjacent to the derelict farmhouse, where fourteen IRA gunmen died in a shootout with crown forces early last month. Mr Lee, whose family has farmed extensively in the area for generations, had a single gunshot wound to his head. Police believe he was foully murdered by the IRA. However, they refused to confirm reports that a notice, accusing Mr Lee of being a 'crown informer, responsible for the murders of the fourteen Curramore volunteers on August 3$^{rd,}$' was found beside the body.*

## The Doormat

'If you don't behave yourself, May Reardon,' my mother would threaten me, when I was child, 'a ghost will carry you off in the middle of the night and you'll never be seen or heard of again.'

I'm reminded of that now, sitting here, looking at my husband pottering around the kitchen. God knows, if anyone deserves to be haunted, it's Dick Sheridan. I can hardly believe the things I'm after finding out about that man. I mean, forty years almost I've spent with this, this, *bastard, and* do you know, I realise now, that I've never known the man at all? Isn't that a shocking thing to have to admit - after all this time? Four children we've reared and he running around after anything in a skirt the whole time? And for the last ten years, hasn't he been keeping another woman in a small flat in Dublin?

And *I* neve*r* found out until three months ago. Imagine that! So there he is now, my double-crossing, cheating husband, sitting opposite, aftershave smothering me, green chinos and mustard shirt, a mustard shirt mind you, at his age! Off to meet HER, of course. And to think that for years, I believed every word that came out of that lying bastard's mouth.

'Oh, May, Declan and myself must make up a foursome at Lahinch at the weekend,' he'd say or

'Oh May, would you believe, myself and Frankie are after making it to the final of the squash tournament in Dublin? So we'll have to overnight, but I'll make it up to you, love, we'll go out for a nice meal at that new Italian when I come back,' How could anyone be so *blind*?

Of course, I understand it all now when it's far too late to do anything about it. As clear as day, I can see that I just never got over the shock of Dick Sheridan marrying me all those years ago - Dick Sheridan who could have anyone in the parish, choosing *me*, plain May Reardon. Hindsight is great thing. Shure, I was so bloody grateful I never got over it, let him walk all over me. A career doormat, that's me. My God, he must have many a laugh at poor gullible May. And all the time, the fancy woman in the small flat in Dublin with her size ten figure and her designer clothes even if her face, now that I've seen it close up, has more plaster work done on it than our sun-room wall.

So how *did* I find out about him? Well, I died, that's how. A heart attack! Can you credit that? Me, May Sheridan, who never smoked or drank in her life! And a cheating husband wasn't the only thing I discovered, the other revelation was finding out how bloody useless ghosts are!

Ghosts, hah, how are you? I can woo, hoo and boo, hoo and run around the house, making faces and screaming and waving my hands, until the cows come home, but shure, if the bastard can't see or hear me, what is the bloody point?

Jesus, I'd die from the shame of it - if I wasn't already dead!

# Turn the Ship and Away We Go

It had been the best summer for years. Day after day, the sun shone and small clouds tripped across the blue sky. Not a hint of rain. Even the older farmers bringing churns of milk to the creamery never remembered a summer like it. It was like Africa, they told each other, though they couldn't know that, never having been there. But they all nodded in agreement, perspiring in their woollen shirts and heavy trousers while the horses flicked away the flies and longed to move out of the heat into the coolness of the covered back-stand of the creamery.

The tar on the road blistered and burst and the river, a long narrowing finger of water, trickled through the parched, lifeless fields on either side of it before falling gratefully into the coolness of the glen just over a mile outside the village. The Glen of the Horses, though no one from the village ever called it that. As long as anyone could remember, it had always been known as Gleann na gCapall, mysterious and gloomy. Once, long, long ago, a man, driving a team of horses before him had ploughed out the glen from hostile rock as a punishment for angering the gods.

When Josie was a young girl growing up in the village, she felt so sorry for that poor man and wondered what awful thing he had done to merit such a terrible punishment. When she was young, too, she knew, like all the villagers and their children, that the Hairy Boy- O lived in Gleann na gCapall and watched out for bold boys and girls so that he could spirit them away into the darkness of the glen where they were never seen again. So she and the other children took great care not to be too bold and it must have worked, because not one child was ever taken by the Hairy Boy- O when she was growing up in the village.

And the summer days passed, tumbling over each other in a blaze of dappled sunshine. Walking up the grassy avenue to the derelict big house outside the village, her mother held her by the hand and sang, the notes rising and weaving and floating into the sweeping branches of the huge trees lining both sides of the avenue.

She wondered if the fairies lived in the trees and bushes but when she asked, her mother simply laughed and caught her by her two hands, sweeping them both onto the middle of the moss lined avenue to play her favourite game. Hands crossed diagonally with her mother's, they both skipped along, her small feet flying,

Hi ho, tipsy toe,

Turn the ship

And away we go o o o.

When they came to 'turn the ship and away we go' she squealed in delight. As her mother swung her round to the other side, her feet left the dust covered road and flew into the air, before landing again, bare feet plopping into the soft, fresh cowpat, made by Dinny Kelleher's cows.

When she awakes now, she is smiling. The words still tumble round and round in her head. Now, filled with the scent of summer, lips quiver the words of the childhood rhyme silently while the sun's rays dance and whirl through the open window, darting teasingly even into the narrowest corners, before tripping back out again. The blue and yellow flowers in the glass vase trap the dancing stripples of light carrying the sweet smell of summer into the long narrow room and bringing her back to the small village of her childhood almost seventy years ago.

It had been summer, too, that morning long ago, her last morning at home, the summer she'd turned seventeen. The sun played hide and seek amongst the branches of the holly tree and mosaics of light and shade quivered and shifted on the narrow path leading up to her grandmother's cottage. The iron bath, all soapy water and dirty shirts, lay to the side of the open door and Granny's bloomers, pink and white coconut creams, waved from the clothes line between the timber poles. Jack kept the engine of his hackney running as she ran before her mother up the path to the open door of the cottage.

Granny, round in a blue polka dot apron, smelling of carbolic and apples, pulled her into her arms in a medley of muffled words, chest expanding and contracting like a concertina. There was no trace of Uncle Mick, except for his dirty football sock under the armchair, The Sacred Heart on the wall, the white net curtains and the small crack on the squat white jug with Nash's Lemona.., the de had vanished years ago.

Her grandmother had pushed a paper bag into her hand – three cakes of warm soda bread, she said, and something small from Uncle Mick. Later, she'd found the creased envelope with a bright pink ten- shilling note and rubbed it with her fingers over and over. A final shuddering hug and out again by the soapy bath almost falling over Rosie, a madcap exclamation mark of moving fur and waving tail, skidding round the corner. She felt the lick on her bare legs and bent down to pat her head but missed and met the air instead. Outside the blue gate, Birdie Hayes, from across the fields, shuffled in the dust beside the Ford Anglia motor car. Not the full shilling, Birdie, they said. His only song, Danny Boy, tinny voice lost beyond the middle rows at the village Christmas concerts.

'Ah, Jasus Birdie, can't you sing up, man? Sing up.'

Now, one hand on the bonnet, with the other he touched his cap.

'Don't, don't be, be, ffforgetting us out there now, Josie'

As the car eased off, she knelt on the tan leather seats and looked and looked and Granny and Rosie and Birdie and the holly tree all wobbled up and down in a bubble of tears and breaking sun. Thirstily, she drank it all in, that last drive - past the faded red brick school and the room where Sr. Benizi spoke to the girls in the confirmation class. The sums and the suffering and Miss Power with her swinging hand and thick ankles pouring over polished brown laced shoes.

'Ring a ring of rosies,

A pocket full of posies

Atishoo, atishoo,

And we all fall down.

Just outside the village, Paddy Pudding, (for years, she had thought that Pudding was his second name) traipsed along the road with a gabháil of sticks. He stopped at the sound of the engine and moved further onto the grass verge, then waved his hands at the moving car, slowly, sticks and all, like a benediction.

At Newcastle West Railway Station, the crowds of people bewildered her but her eyes only on her mother, for the last time, and her heart breaking, breaking. The heat of her mother's body as she held her close and the faint smell of mothballs from her summer dress. Then her mother's hand, soft and slow, moved up and down her cheek as she spoke over her head to the tall figure in black standing quietly aside.

'Take good care of my girl now, Sr. Margaret. Shure, she's only a child still.'

And the train's loud belching as it pulled out of the station and she looked out the window, still feeling on her cheek the warmth of her mother's hand. She waved and waved and her mother, one hand raised and the other touching her lip, waved back, overflowing eyes on hers, getting smaller and smaller until the train chugged around the bend and her mother was left behind, farther and farther behind and the wheels of the train shouted Stop, Stop and her heart broke into tiny pieces and somersaulted around in her chest.

At last, on the quayside, she stared at the huge ship, climbing up into the heavens. Bewildered and dry eyed, she stood among the crowds, a tangle of horses and carts and shouts and funny smells. Bags and boxes ready for loading and knots of young men and women, some not much older than herself, many clutching cardboard cases.

'Emigrants, may God be good to them,' Sister Margaret said, 'taking the boat to Liverpool, or maybe going to America, to New York or Boston or Oregon'

'Are we emigrants too, Sister?'

'Ah, not in the same way, child, not in the same way''

She looked at the faces, parcels of heartbreak and hope, waiting in line, to be carried out on the tide like so many messages in a bottle. What would their lives be like, she wondered - labouring on railway lines or in noisy, cluttered cities or herding sheep in prairies of loneliness under the Oregon stars? She tried to imagine, from the stories she'd heard in the village - but couldn't. Then, she tried to imagine her own future, in the convent in New South Wales in upside down Australia but couldn't do that either.

In the fading sun of late evening, Roche's Point winked her goodbye. Sr. Margaret's dimpled hands rested lightly on the railings and overhead, gulls cackled and flip flapped in the breath of the wind. Strangely, of all the dead voices left behind, it was Birdie's she heard as the 'SS. Queensland' rolled down the estuary.

Oh Danny Boy, the pipes, the pipes are calling

From glen to glen and down the mountain side

The summer's gone and all the roses dying

'tis you 'tis you must go and I must bide.

It is winter now in New South Wales and although late evening, the sun is still warm. Inside the convent of St. Joseph, the small bedroom is cool and airy. Sister Mary Catherine stares dreamily at the flickering haloes of light on the wall. When she'd woken a short time before, she had wondered for a moment where she was, Birdie's voice was so clear, she had looked around in confusion to see where he was. Then she remembered and smiled faintly. Rubbing the brown beads gently, she lies back against the pillows. Strange, after all these years, she can still remember home so vividly – particularly that last morning. July 27$^{th}$. 1951, when she'd left behind all that she'd loved and set off on her long one-way voyage for the mission fields of Australia as a seventeen - year old postulant. So long ago.

For a long while she lies there in the silence, dreamily watching the dancing light on the bedroom wall, remembering. - lips moving soundlessly.

The summer's gone and all the roses dying

'tis you, 'tis you must go and I must bide…

# The Homecoming

Peter O Neill paced up and down the small neat kitchen of *Fuchsia Cottage*. When he had rearranged the curtains for what must have been the tenth time Teresa, his sister, couldn't stay silent any longer. 'For heaven's sake, man,' she'd scolded,' will you sit down for a minute and stop foostering?' But her tone was affectionate as she guided him to the back door of the cottage.' Look, go out and have a walk around the garden', she ordered ' t'will relax you, if nothing else,' The look he gave her was both apologetic and grateful and giving his arm a small squeeze, she watched with a fond smile as he disappeared down the garden path.

Had he been this nervous the first time? Peter didn't remember, it was a long time ago. Stretching back on the red garden seat, he let the soft rustling of the trees and the heat of the sun on his face, gradually soothe him.

At 68, Peter O Neill was still a fine looking man. Tall and thin, with his silver hair combed back neatly, he could well have passed for a man twenty years younger. He had only returned home to the small village of Curramore the previous year after spending most of his adult life in England. With barely a penny to his name, he had left home, like so many others, in the 1950s and arrived in Manchester where a former neighbour had got him a start in the building trade.

Those first few years were tough and there was more than one occasion when loneliness had almost forced him to pack it all in and return home on the first boat out of Liverpool. But he was stubborn and had his pride. He thought of coming back to the village and to the small cottage where his father and mother could barely make ends meet as it was, and he gritted his teeth and got on with it.

Every few weeks, he'd send a few bob home with a short letter, deliberately upbeat, telling them what a great place Manchester was and how much money a fella could make there if he was willing to work hard and stay out of the pubs. That last bit was true enough. There was plenty work and more money than he'd ever seen in his life. But the pubs were a curse, he'd seen so many young men, lonely and lost, take to the drink so that they could face each day in the large, teeming city where they knew no one. He was determined to avoid being sucked into that so he worked hard and long and every summer, until first his mother, and a few years later his father, had passed away, he'd headed back to Ireland for a few weeks, catching up with family and gossip. After they died, home wasn't the same and he went less often, once every two or three years. He found, too, that most of the lads he grew up with had themselves taken the boat to England and he was more likely to meet them on the building sites around Manchester and Birmingham than he was in the small village at home.

As the years passed, he grew more at home in England and then he met Eileen at a dance in the Irish Club in Manchester. She was from Mayo and had been in England almost five years working as a maid with a wealthy family in the affluent suburb of Sneinton. They'd clicked straight away and were married three years later, settling down in a small terraced house just outside Manchester, where'd they'd lived for the rest of their married life. They'd had no family, much to their regret but they didn't allow what couldn't be to dominate their lives. Cliché and all as it was, they had each other and they were happy. As the years passed, they'd bought their house from the corporation and enjoyed themselves a bit now that they weren't watching the pennies. They'd joined the bowling club, went hill walking and every so often, they'd go back to visit the relations in Mayo and Curramore. They'd even gone to Spain a few times, Peter hadn't liked it much, he preferred being at home, putting his feet up by his own fireside to being roasted alive in Spain. Thank

God, Eileen never minded, she'd laughed at him, affectionately calling him her old stick in the mud.

And then two months after he retired came the dreadful shock of Eileen's death. There she was, sitting opposite him at breakfast one minute, talking and drinking a cup of tea and the next, she'd fallen sideways and was gone, just like that. A massive heart attack, the doctor said, there was nothing anyone could have done. In the beginning, Peter had been too heart-broken and shocked to do anything for weeks, except wander around the house in a daze. Then he'd forced himself out to meet friends but it simply wasn't the same, not without Eileen. He went back to Ireland for a holiday three years after she died, saw the small cottage for sale in the village and decided on a whim that he couldn't still explain, to make a complete break and return home.

In Peter's young days, the cottage had belonged to Master O Boyle, the schoolteacher. The house was spotless and big enough for his needs now that he was alone but it was the garden he fell in love with. Neatly trimmed hedges bordered by colourful flowerbeds and apple trees and a little pond in the middle with a red garden seat beside it. The day he saw it, the sunlight danced lazily through the branches of the trees overlooking the garden and he felt an immediate pull. So on impulse he bought it and within three months, everything sold up in England, he had moved in, lock, stock and barrel to *Fuchsia Cottage.*

It had taken him a while to settle. It was one thing to come back for a few weeks in the summer but living there permanently was different. At first, he hardly knew what to do with himself and thought he'd made a dreadful mistake. Many of the villagers were newcomers, busy young people, working in the nearby town. But gradually, he'd persevered and got chatting to people over a pint in the local or buying his messages in the local Quik Pick. He'd joined the Senior Citizens' Club and the Gardening Circle and made friends there too. The Senior Citizens' Club was very active and had a busy social schedule organising trips to such places as Bunratty Castle and Croke Park. They'd even visited Dáil Eireann and Aras an Uachtaráin where they met the President. Once or twice a month, in his small car, he visited his younger sister, Teresa, who lived only an hour or so from Curramore. With the clubs and the gardening, he was kept busy and in the twelve months since he'd settled there, had become part of the fabric of village life.

At night in the silence of the cottage though, Peter admitted that despite his friends and his outings and his garden, he was still lonely. Lonely for companionship and someone to talk to, someone with whom he could share his thoughts and have a bit of a laugh with– like he'd done with Eileen. He'd sighed, well, that only happened once in a lifetime, he thought and gave himself a mental shake. 'For goodness sake, man, stop feeling sorry for yourself,' he'd admonished himself, 'Count your blessings, there's many a man that would be happy to step into your shoes,' So he counted his blessings and if, at times, he felt an ache of loneliness stealing over him, he ignored it and got on with his life.

'That was fascinating,' the voice had a soft Northern burr and Peter turned to find himself facing a well -dressed woman in her sixties, a woman he'd never seen before. She had bright blue eyes and was smiling at him. They'd just been listening to a talk by the well- known landscape gardener, Joe Sheridan – a talk Peter had been looking forward to enthusiastically and he hadn't been disappointed. The man had been inspirational and had so fired Peter up that he now forgot his customary shyness in front of women.

'Wonderful,' he agreed enthusiastically' I can't wait to try out a few of those ideas of his for shady corners'

'I can't either,' the stranger confessed 'such simple ideas too, that's the beauty of it'.

They chatted for a few minutes and then Peter held out his hand.

'Peter O Neill,' he said.

'Muriel O Reilly,' the woman took his outstretched hand.

'Look,' Peter said, looking around and noticing that people were beginning to make their way to the kitchen where refreshments were being served 'maybe, if you're not hurrying away, we could grab a cup of tea and a cake?'

'Why not,' Muriel agreed.

In an unusual show of gallantry for the shy Peter, he held out his arm which Muriel took laughingly. That night they'd talked for what seemed like hours. Peter hadn't realised what a huge gap Eileen's death had left in his life. He'd spoken more, he reckoned later, in those couple of hours, than he'd done for the previous six months. Muriel was a widow, she'd told him and originally from Holywood, in County Down. She was in Curramore visiting her sister, Esther, who was married a mile or so outside the village. Peter knew her sister by sight, but hadn't ever had the opportunity to speak to her or her husband. Muriel, herself, had married a Wexford man and settled down in Gorey, her husband Bill's home town, where they'd lived for almost forty years until Bill's death two years before. She told him about her two grown up children, Sean, working in Brussels and Marie in London. With both children away, Muriel had found herself lonely and unsettled after Bill's death. 'You feel like a spare part, rattling round the kitchen,' she'd confessed to Peter, who agreed whole-heartedly. He and Eileen hadn't been blessed with children, he'd told Muriel, a hint of regret in his voice when Muriel told him of how close she and her children were and of their frequent visits home. Muriel was so easy to talk to that it was with a shock that Peter realised that most of the people had left for home and Tom, the caretaker of the hall where the Gardening Circle held their talks, was waiting to lock up and go home.

Well, after meeting Muriel, he'd had a new lease of life. They'd begun spending more and more time together. No longer was the cottage a lonely place, it echoed with the sound of chatter and laughter. Muriel, like Eileen was so easy to be around and they shared so many interests, gardening, walking – they even liked the same type of music and books. When Peter asked Muriel to marry him and she accepted, nobody in the village, except perhaps, Peter himself, was surprised.

Peter brought himself back to the present. Goodness, had he actually dozed off? To his surprise, he no longer felt nervous and when he rose from the seat, it was with a sense of purpose and confidence. In less than an hour, in front of family and friends at the small village church, he and Muriel would be married. As he hurried up the path, eager now for the ceremony to begin, he imagined he felt the spirit of Eileen smiling down at him approvingly.

## The Grafter

Christ, he was getting too old for this, Vinnie thought as he crouched in a huddle of trees above the car park of *Knapp's Inn* in Balbriggan. He thought of his youthful ambition –to do a *Ronnie Biggs* and retire to the Bahamas. Well, no, not the Bahamas, too hot and Vinnie couldn't stand the heat –brought him out in hives. He shuddered. No, definitely not the Bahamas. Somewhere nearer home, like Howth maybe.

When the moon was hidden behind the clouds again, he cautiously clambered down the steep wooded incline behind the pub, clutching a small magalite. Suddenly he stopped, pointing his torch downwards. Ah, for fuck's sake. He nearly puked. His brand new trainers were covered in fresh dog shit. If there was one thing Vinnie couldn't stand beside hives and the heat of the Bahamas, it was fresh fucking dog-shit. He felt his stomach heave and quickly turned, wiping off the slime in a patch of grass before resuming his awkward descent towards the car park

Then he was there, the dark shadow of the *Knapp Inn* looming out of the darkness before him. He edged his way along the back wall and came to the window he'd unlatched earlier. Bingo! Vinnie grinned smugly as he greased himself through the small opening.

Christ, it was small though. It hadn't looked that bleeding small from the inside. Panicking, he shoved and pushed and suddenly a loud tearing noise broke the silence as the arse of his pants ripped and he could feel the soft gush of air fanning his lower regions. Fuck. He shoved again and a fresh wave of panic rolled over him as he found he couldn't advance any further. Jesus Christ, he was stuck, too far in to come out and too far out to get in. Small beads of sweat popped out on his forehead. Christ, he'd be stuck there till someone found him in the morning, arse out through his pants and probably smothered by the fumes of the dog shit off his new trainers. He could see the tabloid headlines already. The awful thought of being on the front page galvanised him and with a sudden swivel, he was free.

Minutes later or so it felt to Vinnie, he was back in the safety of the huddle of trees. Breathlessly, he threw his booty on the ground and bent to examine it. But the next time the moon sailed out from behind the clouds, Vinnie didn't even notice – there he stood, a dumpy middle aged man, a hole in the arse of his striped tracksuit pants, new trainers ruined with fresh dog shit and his shoulders scratched and bleeding from forcing himself through a window he was far too fat for.

Christ Almighty, he hadn't even broken even. What was in the *Support North Dublin's Dogs Home* wouldn't even cover the cost of the bleeding runners he'd spent 30 quid on in Penny's. He kicked *St Ita's Hospital for the Aged* viciously into the blanket of darkness and sent *Alms for the African Missions* swiftly after it and with a last bitter look towards the empty car - park disappeared into the bushes.

'*Knapp's Inn*,' he muttered '*Knapp's* bloody *Inn*, me arse – Crap's fucking Inn, more like'. The muttering faded and when the moon next chanced to peep out from behind the clouds, there was nothing to be seen – well, nothing except half a dozen kicked in charity boxes and a freshly squashed dog turd, under the huddle of trees above the sleeping inn.

# Voices from Afar

The voices are never still. I have no peace. When I fall into an exhausted sleep, I can still hear them – low, pleading, incessant. impossible to ignore, though I try desperately to drown them out. I put my hands to the side of my head and shake it from side to side in a frenzy. I pull the hair growing there until I yelp with pain but all my efforts are futile, the voices are audible still. I shiver now, remembering the long years spent on the mountain, the bitter winds coming from the sea, the cold mist frozen tentacles, taunting, caressing me in a deathly embrace. I saw no one then, except the man, surly and monosyllabic, tangled hair blowing wildly around a face that never smiled.

I will not return to that wretched place; I vow I will not. I will not.

It was a glorious evening, the last one I spent among my own people. The sun, a ball of flame, sinking in the west, the bonfire, huge and crackling, flames licking the air. My mouth watered as I stared at the boar, slowly roasting on the spit. There was the sound of many voices, carefree laughter, children darting forward towards the flames, then retreating, squealing with delighted terror.

It was strange. Thinking back now, one would think there would be some hint of danger. Should we not have felt a frisson of alarm, a sense of foreboding? But there was nothing, no hint of what was to come. Even as I stood there, they were approaching ever closer, their boat riding the waves noiselessly, wild-eyed, ruthless, faces tight, focusing on their mission.

They attacked in the middle of our merry-making. Our village was completely unprepared for these dark strangers from across the sea. Laughter turned to terrified cries, as boys and girls, just like me were grabbed in strong, determined arms. The old were left untouched. Our menfolk tried to protect us, to stop the marauders but they were no match for the men from across the sea.

 I couldn't move. My feet were anchored to the earth. I watched, helpless, unable to flee as the raiders went about their evil work. Then, I was roughly caught from behind by a grunting man, who spoke in a rough guttural voice. I struggled frantically but it was futile. He was too strong, too powerful. "Father, Father." I found my voice but I could not be heard above the mayhem and bedlam all round me. Besides, who was to help me? We were utterly overpowered. Then, I felt a hard knock on my head and knew no more.

 When I came to, I felt sick and groggy. My head ached. My feet and arms were bound, tight, painfully tight. There was something large, a rag I think, stuck into my mouth to prevent me making a sound. I moved my head, and could make out several others, all bound like me. At first, I could not make out where I was, what was happening. Then, I felt the swell underneath me. We were on the sea. Terror crept into my bones, the very pores of my skin. My heart pounded and I whimpered, as silent tears made their way down my cheek as I thought of Father and Mother. Where were they? What had happened to them? Were they safe? I knew I would not see them again.

 I must have nodded off or drifted into unconsciousness because the next thing I remember is being pulled to my feet and shoved forward, stumbling as I climbed a flimsy rope ladder. Rough hands hauled me onto a quayside. I blinked. My eyes and ears were assaulted by a cacophony of movement and noise. A throng of bearded men and boys dressed in robes shouted in a strange tongue. Cattle, sheep and pigs milled around, the stench was overpowering.

From the nods and gestures, it was clear that my companions and I were the subject of the conversation, they pointed at us and guffawed, some turned their backs and spat, a few advanced and stood looking at us as if we were cattle. They had long shaggy hair and coarse, unkempt beards. They were huge men. They poked and prodded at us, biting out strange words to our captor. I felt faint and swayed on my feet.

One by one, my companions were led away until only I was left. My captor uttered something violently and hit me across the head. I swayed and would have fallen but I was caught by an enormous man in a short cape. I looked up, dazed, his eyes were grey and as cold as the winter seas. He spoke quietly to my captor, who grimaced. Their speech became more rapid, more animated. Then my captor raised his shoulders in a shrug. The man with the cold grey eyes pointed at me and beckoned. The last I saw of my captor, he was struggling to drive two goats onto the boat bobbing gently on the water.

Events blurred. I recall being taken on a long journey. We rested every so often, eating rough bread and cheese washed down by water that the stranger carried in a pack on his mule. He rode and I walked until I stumbled from fatigue and he gestured roughly that I mount the other mule. At last, after climbing steadily for what seemed an age, we arrived at a vast open field where pigs roaming freely.

The stranger pushed me, roughly, from the mule and gestured to follow him. He took me to a wooden structure, where there was lots of straw, he pointed at troughs in the field, then at the pigs and then at the straw. There was a lot more gesturing, he pointed to me and the wooden structure. Suddenly, it hit me, this was now my home. I was to stay here, the structure was my dwelling and my duty was to care for the pigs. He gave me a rough brown robe and turning on his heels, walked in the direction whence we had come. I watched as he mounted the mule and disappeared into the mist that was slowly coming in from the mountain. And the realisation dawned - I was a slave in a foreign country with no hope of escape.

Many suns rose and fell, many mists rolled down from the mountain-side. I shivered and tried to keep count of the days. The stranger came sometimes with food for the pigs and me. Sometimes I was so hungry I ate some of the animals' food and all the time I prayed God not to forsake me. I had counted 2,190 days when deliverance came. In a dream, I saw an angel who told me that I had to escape. Her directions were so vivid and concise that when I woke, I remembered them perfectly. Was I losing my mind after all that time in the wilderness, with no one to talk to? Perhaps. But my mind was made up, I would follow the directions of the angel and take my chances, so bidding farewell to the pigs who did not seem unduly affected by my departure, I turned my back on the mountain and set out for the sea.

All that is light years away now. I need not say how miraculous, how joyful my return was to my family and friends. Mother and Father were alive. They had long thought me dead and lost to them and were overcome at my sudden appearance among them. I resumed my life and in time, God called me to do His work and I was consecrated a priest.

I was happy – until the voices began, calling me back, begging, pleading, 'Come back,' they called, their voices echoing eerily across the water that separated us.

I put my hands against my ears and wept.

## Wedding preparations

It was actually Peggy who spotted the poster below in the library window, during her weekly knitting circle morning. Mavis, our local librarian is only brilliant at organising all sorts of activities for every age group in our local branch. We've had rap bands, writers' talks, talks on how to grow your own yams, some sort of yoga from Pakistan, Indian meditation, Far Eastern meditation, Zen mindfulness and oh, God only knows what else. We've had everything in that library, bar Sliabh Luachra set dancing, psychic readings and séances. Although Peggy claims that one morning when she was doing a row of purl, the table moved. I wouldn't set much store on that bit of information though as the whole village knows that building was thrown up in about six weeks during the Celtic Tiger years by Baldy Biggane, the Fianna Fáil TD, who's in the construction business. Whenever anyone mentions Baldy and construction in the same sentence, Peggy nearly gets apoplectic, rolling her eyes to heaven in the most grotesque fashion and ranting on about destruction, brown envelopes, corruption and the planning system. And of course, this being Peggy, we have to have a spiel about the brave men and women of 1916 and how the heroes above in the GPO, must be only turning in their graves, at the shoneens and the gobshites running the country now. She says all this without pausing for breath even. Jesus!

To be honest, part from swallowing Mikado biscuits like she's been on hunger strike for a week and upsetting the spirits enough for them to start messing around with the tables, I'm not quite sure what Peggy actually does down at the library every Wednesday morning. I mean, I haven't seen anything like a finished product and she's been part of the knitting group now for at least eighteen months. Wouldn't any normal person have half a dozen blankets knitted in that amount of time, for Christ's sake? As far as I can make out, it's a pure gossip shop and the needles and all their talk about fancy stitches are only for show. Peggy and Lourda came near to putting each other's eyes out only the other week with the needles, in a row over Brexit, and only for Mavis coming between them, God only knows what would have happened. That poor woman must be a walking saint to put up with Peggy and that Lourda Kennefick in the same room.

But to get back to the point I wanted to make. Ah, the point about the poster Peggy saw below in the library window, shure what other point is there? You see, Dolores's only daughter Imelda, is getting married next year to some doctor working above in Beaumont, and Peggy, Bridie, Marilyn and myself are all shoe-ins for an invite to the wedding. Well, Peggy says that many's the time she wiped that girl's arse when she was in nappies and it would be a right slap in the face if she, Peggy, didn't get an invitation. She got right aggressive, saying that whatever about anyone else, (meaning me, Bridie and Marilyn, of course) she had certainly earned her right to be there, and if she wasn't invited, neither Dolores nor Imelda nor the fancy Beaumont doctor she's marrying, would ever put a foot inside her door in the future, blah, blah, blah. Jesus, I wouldn't mind, but the wedding is not till next summer, for feck's sake.

Anyway, Dolores put Peggy out of our misery by saying the whole lot of us were going to be asked. It's going to be a right posh do, according to Dolores, the whole thing is taking place in Dromoland Castle. Well, that got our attention alright, I can tell you. We were all in great form, sitting outside on my patio, drinking wine and toasting Imelda and Harold (the fiancé, the fiancé, shure, who did you think Harold was?) in fact, we toasted everyone in both families. I think the evening ended with us toasting the Minister for Health, but my memory is none too clear on this point....

It was the following morning, in the cold light of day, that the reality hit us! I was barely up when Peggy arrives in with a face on her that would stop a clock and the kettle was only just boiled when the other three appeared, looking as tragic as Theresa May on the steps of Downing Street, when she was trying to persuade the whole world that she'd won the election. It was Bridie who summed up our dilemma most clearly. 'Jesus,' says she and she waving the mug of scalding coffee dangerously close to my head 'we're going to be a holy show below in Dromoland Castle, in front of all the doctors from Beaumont, shure the four of us are like a herd of heifers after being fattened up to be taken into the factory.'

There was a short pause and then, all of us slowly put down the ginger snap biscuits we were about to bite into and looked at ourselves. I mean, really looked at ourselves. It was Peggy who broke the awful silence.

'There's a notice below in the library window,' says she 'for something called HEAVENLY BODIES SLIMMING CAMP. It said something about maximum weight and minimum pain.'

There was another long silence as we contemplated the immediate future and the attaining of the heavenly bodies.

To cut a long story short, the whole lot of us are going down to the community centre tomorrow night, to sign up for the classes. Shure, what choice have we? We can't be waddling into, like, Dromoland Castle, swaddled in rolls of fat and making fools of ourselves.

I have a strong gut feeling this could be a very long year.

Printed in Great Britain
by Amazon